Gordon Shand had an unremarkable and sheltered upbringing in the countryside. At school, he had a rebellious period playing the class clown until slowly reaching maturity, where he enrolled and studied at a university. Graduating with an honour's degree in philosophy, he opted for a career completely unrelated to the skills he had acquired previously – the whisky industry. One decisive winter, with the deterioration of his mental health, he conceived of the very tales that are to follow.

Gordon Shand

ASYLUM

AUSTIN MACAULEY PUBLISHERS™
LONDON * CAMBRIDGE * NEW YORK * SHARJAH

Copyright © Gordon Shand 2022

The right of Gordon Shand to be identified as author of this work has been asserted by the author in accordance with section 77 and 78 of the Copyright, Designs and Patents Act 1988.

All rights reserved. No part of this publication may be reproduced, stored in a retrieval system, or transmitted in any form or by any means, electronic, mechanical, photocopying, recording, or otherwise, without the prior permission of the publishers.

Any person who commits any unauthorised act in relation to this publication may be liable to criminal prosecution and civil claims for damages.

This is a work of fiction. Names, characters, businesses, places, events, locales, and incidents are either the products of the author's imagination or used in a fictitious manner. Any resemblance to actual persons, living or dead, or actual events is purely coincidental.

A CIP catalogue record for this title is available from the British Library.

ISBN 9781528946209 (Paperback)
ISBN 9781528946216 (Hardback)
ISBN 9781528971676 (ePub e-book)
ISBN 9781398418448 (Audiobook)

www.austinmacauley.com

First Published 2022
Austin Macauley Publishers Ltd®
1 Canada Square
Canary Wharf
London
E14 5AA

Chapter 1
Origins

I am here, alone, yet surrounded. Drawing nearer, my opposers, identifiable only by the means of imagination. I gasp for air, avert my eyes, and wait for my impending demise. I know not where I am or where I shall go. My pursuers intent inconceivable but presence intimidating, I muster the courage to overcome my fate and flee. Out of the void of darkness a light appears, shielding my eyes I cautiously approach it. I see a tiny object, reminiscent of the depictions of an atomic nucleus, suspended in mid-air. Overcome with curiosity I touch the object. An efflux of energy pulsates through my finger surging up my arm to my body. Distracted by this anomaly I failed to see the bright particle in the distance on a collision course. It strikes and the resultant blast wave propels me through the air as my flesh ignites and is incinerated. I feel no pain but have a heightened awareness of the unrelenting conservation of energy. A foreboding dark blotch appears in the inferno - instantly I fear the singularity, expanding at an unfathomable rate, absorbing the aftermath of the ionized plasma, light, and infrared radiation, growing all the while in magnitude. The final act, the consumption of all. The apocalyptic totality necessitates the negation of reality until I emerge from the unconscious ordeal, trembling. Bewildered momentarily by the encounter, I breathe a sigh of relief that the comfort of banal existence has returned, and the great void has evaporated. Avoiding psychoanalytic interpretation of the intangible experience, I slip on my slippers and make my way to the living room. Concluding the self-inflicted torment with concerted suppression, I inhale putrid fumes of a delectable cigarette; a perceived remedy, inessential yet an inescapable necessity, with a dilation of pupils, I exhale. A subsidiary life support, oxygen, floods my lungs and forces what little life I have into the vast expanse of my living room. I must quit this habit. Unfinished, a routine, I must continue, or else suffer like a withering specimen ripe for extinction. A complimentary brew of tea, a quintessential solace in grave times. How my being is now complete, and my dissatisfaction abated.

From hedonism to hygiene, what a life I lead. Cleansed of an afterthought of the day before, I dress for the day ahead. I hesitantly approached the front door, placed my head against it and closed my eyes. I imagined the congested traffic en route to work, the awkward social interactions I was obliged to participate in, and above all else the hinderance the challenges pose at my place of employment. With the mental image streaming through my mind, it compelled me to gently bang my head against the door. I must give the impression that I am not a hopeless misanthrope, put on a smile and charm the objects of antipathy. A brief prelude interrupted my thought, "I may have an extraordinary breakthrough," with an accompanying analgesic effect I yelled out that I can achieve the impossible, that no obstruction shall stop me. I swung open the door and with exceeding alacrity I walked to the car.

I buckled up and wondered why I persistently have that moment of introspection especially since my inner sanctum; the last retreat, is not a benign state where I usually draw optimism from. It is rather a domain of cynicism where even my own motives are met with suspicion by the intrusive personalities eavesdropping on my inner monologue, torturing my psyche with their infernal opinions, dispelling my self-esteem. Those degenerates if only they had physical constitution with a functioning nervous system so I could inflict pain upon them. Alas, I shall admit defeat to these invincible yet insignificant figments of my imagination for the time being with the only consolation that upon my death they too will perish.

The theory itself is tenuous, the formulas incomplete and the application unthinkable but despite this a research laboratory has employed me and is willing to fund the practical aspect of the endeavour, they have even provided me with an attractive assistant. I may as well be an illusionist. But I was worse, I engaged in pseudoscience. As a staunch scientist, I held a great deal of contempt towards the nature of my research and would have ridiculed anyone associated with it, yet I persisted, due to the seductive theoretical outcome. Luckily, I have been provided with the apparatus to perform experimentation to confirm or deny my conjecture. How this opportunity arose, at first, was innocuous – I was lecturing at the university; of course, I stuck to the perfunctory curriculum but the transpiring events whilst on my own recognizance piqued my curiosity. It commenced with the discussion of my theory with Dr Wilde, a fellow of the university, whom I regarded as a dear friend. During these thought-provoking intervals, Dr Wilde invited a Dr Scholtz to join in our debate, according to Dr Wilde, Dr Scholtz was an old post graduate buddy who showed a great deal of interest in unorthodox areas of research. He displayed a great enthusiasm for my theory and invited me to the corporate headquarters where he had the lofty position of the chief executive officer. I had no prior knowledge of its existence.

Before I could be given the grand tour, I had to sign a non-disclosure agreement.

"Why didn't you blind fold me and throw me into an unmarked van?"

"That would be a drastic measure, Dr Barrett. This is just a minor precaution."

"Very well."

I signed the document and we got underway with the tour.

"This is impressive, Dr Scholtz."

In matter of fact, it was a fairly nondescript laboratory. I was disappointed.

"This is our pharmaceutical department, it is a commercial business licensed to research, develop, market and distribute drugs, for the purpose of healthcare."

"You are quite the beguiling fellow, luring me here, but I am surprised it is for the sake of Pharmacology. I was hoping it would be in the context of our debate."

"I am a man of many talents, Dr Barrett."

I was ushered into the restricted area which was conspicuously sign posted on the door. We walked through a corridor, entered an elevator, and descended two floors.

"I fail to see how this is relevant to my theory?"

"Be patient Dr Barrett. I have something to show you. Right through that door, go ahead."

He motioned me through.

"Incredible, is that a nuclear reactor?"

"Yes, take a moment to comprehend the implications."

"You're going to grant me access to do experimentation?"

"That's the idea."

After much deliberation I expressed my concern.

"I am hesitant to undertake an apprenticeship knowing fully well the consequences – of catastrophic proportions, I must add."

"You will be thoroughly taught how to operate the reactor and monitored very closely to prevent any accidents. In addition to this, narrow steel fibres reinforce the concrete increasing the tensile strength of this room containing any lapse of procedure. And one must not forget we are two floors underground."

"That's reassuring. How do you propose to protect me in the event of a core meltdown?

"Go on…"

"If corium is formed in the reactor, melting it in the process and leaking out, the radioactive material will chemically react with all this damn concrete producing high levels of hydrogen, which could potentially cause an explosion, killing me in the process."

"Dr Barrett, we have adopted an innovative solution for such a scenario. If a nuclear fuel element exceeds its melting point, we will inject a granular carbonate mineral into the reactor substantially cooling the corium. It is a far quicker and safer alternative to water. Furthermore, we have a secondary coolant system that comes online if the heat in the reactor exceeds that removed by cooling of the surrounding water so a nuclear meltdown should never occur."

"I presume you install a neutron absorbing material such as Cadmium metal to regulate the rate of reaction?"

"Very astute Dr Barrett; yes, it is a very effective 'neutron poison'."

Sceptical, I walked over to the reactor and gave it a tap for effect.

"Is that thing even functional?"

"Tried and tested."

"And I suppose you just have some highly enriched Uranium lying around?"

"We have a legitimate source."

"Interesting… When do I get started?"

"There are some formalities we have to attend to before you can commence."

"Understandable, you can't just let loose any maniac. Before we proceed, may I ask why a pharmaceutical company has a nuclear reactor in their basement?"

"The board of directors believe we can make advancements in nuclear medicine through the production of radioisotopes for diagnosis and therapy with the application to the treatment of cancer. But don't misconstrue our motive we are not a charitable organisation, and I must insist if you would like to gain employment I suggest you refrain from any further inquest."

"Admirable and duly noted."

I resigned from the University forthwith, in the knowledge that I would receive a higher wage and the opportunity to verify my compulsion. Leaving behind the uncomprehending larvae to feast on the teat of another well-nourished academic. The common simpletons were tolerable, in most cases well mannered. It was the precocious monsters that really infuriated me. Scientific inquiry being integral I never attempted to discourage them from nurturing their own reasoning and methodology, but I did however cunningly and discreetly, without reservation, introduce a confounding variable, and form a counterargument capable of diminishing their ever-growing ego. On the contrary, I am not a sadist, I never took pleasure in this, I merely wanted to prevent society from having to tolerate the schmucks. I digress, did I mention I got a new company car? I made a facetious request for a beautiful Aston Martin and surprisingly Dr Scholtz granted me this. And so, my new venture began.

The ideal vocation took precedence over my suspicions of this organisation masquerading as humanitarian to turn a profit. To begin with, I underwent an intensive training program to master the operation of the reactor. My instructor, Dr Roland Campbell, oblivious to casting aspersions, jovially referred to me as the atomic savant. It was an engaging experience, with frequent moments of laughter, despite the severity of risk. Dr Campbell was one of the few humans I had admiration for. Once adept, I the protege, was given full autonomy and my trusted tutor disappeared. I enquired with Dr Scholtz.

"May I speak with you, Dr Scholtz."

"Out with-it Dr Barrett. I have an urgent meeting I must attend."

"What's the situation with Dr Campbell?"

"He proved to be expendable."

"But he is an invaluable source of information."

"Now you take up that mantle Dr Barrett."

"Your faith in me is completely misplaced, my inexperience will be the cause of a monumental disaster."

"Dr Barrett, your project is one of many, each of which has a senior operator undertaking all the necessary reactor experiments. Are you telling me that you are incapable of working independently? If so, I shall have to reconsider your position."

"I guess not. Sorry for bothering you."

"Excuse me Dr Barrett, I am under a lot of pressure and have forgone my manners. Why don't you come by my office at four thirty for a dram of single malt? I am sure we can resolve any of your concerns."

"Sure, I will see you then."

Despite his reassurance I was inept without Dr Campbell. Through my own investigation into his disappearance, I uncovered a tenuous conspiracy that he was murdered for potentially whistleblowing on the organisation. I, however, had succumbed and felt the extent of the bribery was sufficient to maintaining a level of secrecy about this underground enterprise. Dr Campbell you will not be forgotten but have died in vain. So long, my dear friend.

We had several soft launches but never had I initiated nuclear fission within the reactor and today was the big day. Dr Scholtz accompanied me on this occasion despite my objections that he was endangering his life.

"Preposterous Dr Barrett, I reckon on the effectiveness of Dr Campbell's tutelage, which should be more than adequate for your first trial run, and of course I have faith in you, despite your obvious handicaps, you seem to have an intuitive aptitude for nuclear reactor physics, perhaps an extraordinary gift."

"Contrary to my expectation of a motion of no confidence you seem to be complimenting me although countervailed by belittling connotations, yet I shall adopt your irrational belief as I consider it epistemically innocent, albeit compelling me heedlessly to attaining my objective. Excuse me while I press on with the preparation procedures I have devised."

"Have you deviated from the operations manual?"

"My method is far better than by the book."

"I will disregard your dereliction of duty for I am responsible for giving you full autonomy and therefore take the blame for such a catastrophe that may occur."

"You liberate me with such remarks, Dr Scholtz, and I appreciate how candid you are."

I had enquired with Dr Campbell before he vanished about the mining, enrichment, and fabrication of the fuel for the reactor. I had stressed the importance the insight would have to my calculations.

"You underestimate me, in fact, I'm offended by your condescension. Do you think I would just insert an unknown consistency of fuel into the reactor?"

"I apologise, but the impression you are giving me is that you expect me to do that."

"I will begin by saying that they enrich the Uranium Hexafluoride in a centrifuge. Concentrating the fissile ^{235}Uranium isotope to five percent."

"Fairly standard."

"The enriched Uranium Hexafluoride, in the form of a gaseous substance, is then converted to Uranium Dioxide powder. Subsequently, the powder is pressed and heated into a hard-ceramic material. From there, the pellets are inserted into fuel rods and grouped together into a fuel assembly."

"Again, standard practice."

"Will that suffice for your calculations?"

"In all honesty, no."

"Do accompany me to my office and I will elucidate further."

Returning to the big day, with much elation, I attentively observed the relatively easy task, aided by a hoist mechanism, of installing the fuel assemblies.

"Any damage will be docked from your pay. I jest, it will cost you your lives."

"You certainly know how to choose an opportune time to break the tension, Dr Barrett."

"As long as that is the only thing broken Stevie."

"Of course, governor."

With the imminent realisation of my aspirations, I had to repress my excitement and levity in order to approach, with a keen lucidity, the operation of the reactor without any emotional disturbance. I examined some simple calculations I made to reassure myself of my competence. As is to be expected, I intend to deform and split an atom; harnessing the kinetic energy of the fission fragments, the free neutrons and the fascinating gamma rays which are emitted. To emphasize how asinine the objective is gamma rays are highly penetrating electromagnetic radiation, which are harmful to biological tissue. The method by which we split an atom is to have a fissile material such as ^{235}Uranium and bombard it with low-energy thermal neutrons causing the atoms to absorb a neutron creating an extremely volatile ^{236}Uranium isotope, which splits into two lighter daughter nuclei forming two new comparatively stable elements, ^{141}Caesium and ^{93}Rubidium. What is fascinating and extremely useful is that two neutrons are created in the process which are propelled at other atoms of Uranium causing a fission chain reaction producing a tremendous amount of energy.

I had adopted an idiosyncratic method of determining the energy output of the reactor at an atomic level, first, and subsequently expanding the paradigm to incorporate the proportional quantities to scale. Conveniently, the pre-determined mass of the reactants and products have been established by the extensive research of distinguished scientists of the past. The sum of mass of the pre- and post-atoms and subatomic particles would be subtracted from one another, which would give us an anticipated result, a deficit caused by the binding energy of the Uranium atom nucleus, which is extremely high and exhibits a measurable mass, being removed from the system by fission, in the form of nuclear energy.

One Neutron (1.675×10^{-27} kg) + Uranium (390.173×10^{-27} kg) = 391.848×10^{-27} kg.

Caesium (233.927×10^{-27} kg) + Rubidium (154.248×10^{-27} kg) + two Neutrons (2×1.675) $\times 10^{-27}$ kg = 391.525×10^{-27} kg.

Pre-reactant subtracted by post-product, as follows (391.848×10^{-27} kg) – (391.525×10^{-27} kg) = 3.23×10^{-28} kg.

Having established the mass defect, we can now translate this into the nuclear emission. This is made feasible given that energy and mass are constituents of matter with an intimate relation – the mass of a system is the measure of its energy content. These properties of matter are manifestations of the same thing varying in form and are interchangeable from one another, illustrated by the observation that an objects inertial mass is decreased by emitting energy rendering its resistance to change of motion to be lower. With its application, the deficit of mass has been converted into energy, in particular gamma radiation, which is massless photons, travelling at the speed of light. Thus, energy equals mass multiplied by the speed of light squared given the nature of kinetic energy. Yes, that famous equation that we all familiar with, $E=mc^2$. The speed of light already defined, it is a simple matter of inputting the figures,

3.23×10^{-28}kg $\times (3 \times 10^8)^2$ m/s $= 2.907 \times 10^{-11}$ Joules, which is a derived unit of energy.

Scaling this up to macroscopic proportions, one must divide the weight in grams by the atomic mass and multiply the answer by the number of atoms in twelve grams of ^{12}Carbon (which equals: 1 mole, the unit measure of particles in a substance equivalent to the number of atoms in ^{12}Carbon), known as the Avogadro constant, to ascertain the number of atoms of Uranium in the two kilograms of enriched fuel.

$2,000 / 235.043943 \times 6.02214076 \times 10^{23} = 5.12 \times 10^{24}$ atoms per two kilograms.

Having established the resultant energy from one atom and the number of atoms in two kilograms of Uranium it's a simple case of multiplication.

$2.907 \times 10^{-11} \times 5.12 \times 10^{24} = 148$ trillion Joules per two kilograms of enriched ^{235}Uranium.

To aid in comprehension I will convert joules to megawatts.

148,838,400,000,000 Joules/3,600,000,000 Joules = 41,344 megawatts per hour.

One megawatt is enough to supply the average power requirement for around two thousand homes for an hour. Based on our energy output of the fission reaction in our reactor we should get an outturn capacity that would power approximately eighty-two million homes for an hour. Tremendous. Relative to modern developments in this technology the reactor by design was antiquated but in operation, as a result of the enriched fuel, it exceeded all our expectations with a high rate of efficiency.

Immersed in my calculations, I failed to anticipate the intrusion of Dr Walter Harp, a fellow nuclear scientist, who had decided to drop by.

"Good morning, Dr Scholtz. Good morning, Dr Barrett."

"Morning Dr Harp."

"It looks like you have lost an electron, Dr Barrett."

"What are you talking about?"

"You look positive."

"Very original, Dr Harp."

I looked at Dr Scholtz and I shook my head in disapproval.

"Dr Harp, the opinion of myself and Dr Barrett coincide when I say that we do not enjoy your humour. Now please, step aside and marvel at Dr Barret's mastery."

"I have a wager that you will cause a meltdown on your first attempt."

"Double or nothing?"

"You're on."

"Gambling is not appropriate gentleman, especially in our given circumstance."

"It's a harmless parlay, Dr Scholtz, it's not as if we are gambling with our lives."

I looked at Dr Harp and winked. He returned the gesture.

"That's the fuel assembly installed, Dr Barrett."

"Exceptional work Stevie. Please take your crew and clear the area."

"Thank you, Dr Barrett. Okay, gentleman follow me."

I waited for the subordinate co-conspirators to leave the reactor room before addressing Dr Scholtz.

"I have been meaning to ask Dr Scholtz... Have you had permission to operate this reactor from the office of nuclear regulation?"

"What has prompted this question Dr Barrett?"

"I've been under the impression that this facility is classified for the very reason that it is illegal."

"I smell a conspiracy, Dr Scholtz."

"Be quiet Dr Harp. Dr Scholtz, I must know how you intend to keep this a secret with the number of people involved? There will be serious repercussions and I for one refuse to be incriminated by the testimony of some stooge."

"Listen, that's them now. The authorities are here. Make a run for it, Dr Barrett."

"I'm very serious, Dr Harp."

At that moment, the door swung open, and I nearly jumped out of my skin.

"Forgot my hard hat."

"Holy smokes, Stevie. I thought I was done for."

"Dr Barrett, get a grip of yourself man."

"Sorry, Dr Scholtz. I am suddenly on edge here."

"So, you are able to comprehend that this is a criminal enterprise, and you are a villain?"

"Don't fill his head with nonsense Dr Harp."

"I wouldn't be able to survive imprisonment, Dr Scholtz."

"Dr Scholtz is accurate with his description of you as a special one, panicking about incarceration – pathetic. You're an embarrassment to this organization."

"Okay, Dr Harp that's enough. Dr Barret, it is merely an epistemic property formed through a flawed interpretation of the tangible corporeity your presented with. A warped analytical exaggeration of the subjective status – absent, invalid, and unwarranted. It is in fact an irrational conviction with no probable cause, which your fear amounts to, and for that reason you should calm down and get on with it."

"Your moral turpitude will be met with swift retribution, Dr Harp."

"I meant proceed with the reactor experiment…"

"Not if you intend to uphold that self-righteous attitude, Dr Barrett."

"Gentleman… Please"

"Whatever gave you the impression that I am self-righteous?"

"Your retort, Dr Barrett. Silly, neurotic fool."

"Vile hypocrite, you will get your comeuppance."

"You've got some fight in you, Dr Barrett. I like that; it will serve you well here."

"Did you expect me to react to your arrogance by obediently rolling over so you can tickle my belly?"

"Heel boy."

"I can't adequately express my contempt for you Dr Harp."

"Is this really necessary gentleman?"

"Just assessing the new guy, Dr Scholtz and the verdict is…"

"Hold your tongue Dr Harp. Let me reassure you, Dr Barrett that this facility is licenced and in compliance with the relevant statutory provisions set forth by the office of nuclear regulation. You have nothing to be concerned about. Let's procced Dr Barrett."

"I concede to having no reasonable grounds for suspicion… I will initiate the fission process."

"Good lad."

The abundant ^{238}Uranium isotope in the fuel rods has an auxiliary role in the self-perpetuating reaction. Considered fertile by its occasional nuclear transmutation through neutron capture and beta decay into ^{239}Plutonium – an isotope capable of fission – it serves a purpose in breeder reactors but in our given circumstance it is incidental. Its highly fissile compatriot compensates for its inadequacy. Incapable of spontaneous fission ^{235}Uranium requires a catalyst to get the process moving. A mixture of ^{4}Beryllium and ^{252}Californium is added to the fuel cell. The naturally occurring alpha decay of ^{252}Californium causes alpha particles to escape and when they are absorbed by ^{4}Beryllium further neutrons are released. This provides additional impetus to the bombardment of the ^{235}Uranium nuclei with neutrons. Finally, yet importantly, the integral moderator, which is quite simply blocks of graphite, which slow down neutrons so they can enter the ^{235}Uranium nuclei allowing the chain reaction to commence, preventing them being swallowed up by the more abundant ^{238}Uranium. The fuel assembly was inserted between the graphite by Stevie and his crew. I sat and marvelled at the reactor as the nuclear reaction got underway.

"Nothing like exploiting a natural phenomenon."

"That's the spirit Dr Barrett but be conscious that it is near critical."

"What is a test drive if you can't take it to the extreme, eh, Dr Scholtz?"

"I thought you were safety-conscious, Dr Barrett. Don't exceed the limitations of the reactor for the love of god."

I pumped fresh water into the core coolant system that reactor is submerged in to reduce the temperature which consequently increases the reaction rate. I sat and monitored the sensory apparatus, especially the pressure gauge ensuring that it maintained atmospheric pressure and the temperature of the core was optimal. After some time, content that I have mastered the operation of the reactor I took it the extremities. Bordering on melting point and the reactor on the verge of collapse, I dropped in the Cadmium to absorb neutrons slowing down the reaction and fired up the pumps to the secondary coolant system, halting the activity of the reactor and extinguishing decay heat.

"Dr Barrett that was irresponsible; in fact, downright insane."

"I wasn't far off with my meltdown prediction, that was crazy Dr Barrett."

"You are cognizant of what I am trying to achieve, Dr Scholtz?"

"Of course."

"Then you must appreciate the extent to which I must go."

"It provides little comfort that you appear rational, Dr Barrett. I must insist, if you are going to pull a stunt like that again, ensure that no one else is in the reactor room. I hope to hell our containment measures are sufficient."

"You have my word, Dr Scholtz."

Conceived of through my formative years by the tantalising fantasy of what I would be capable of, I set to work to establish if it is scientifically possible. Whilst at university I made excursions into other subjects for the purpose of corroboration. Reading literature was the primary source, but I also made an effort to attend seminars. The taking of attendance on occasion prevented me from participating but it was mostly my reluctance to accept what the professors had us believe and their dismissal of my preposterous questions, as one kindly remonstrated. I would challenge them and demand they provide further evidence. Their response would be a display of ignoble arrogance, expressing their distaste at my apparent pretensions, conjuring up their authority and banishing me from the classroom. My chosen method of retaliation was to attend their self-indulgent lectures and heckle them. This escalated until the rector was involved and I was threatened with expulsion if I did not behave to the standards expected by students at this prestigious university. I was defeated until I met a neuroscientist in training.

She was remarkable not only in appearance but intellect. She had witnessed one of my spectacles, had mediated the situation as best she could until I had calmed down and reached a plane of sanity. It was not love at first sight from her perspective, I had the impression that she feared me due to my unhinged demeanour. Yet there was an expression of regret on her face for getting involved which caused my heart to melt. I believed she agreed with my approach to these elitist swines but in hindsight, it was most likely an intuition into how she had affected me. Nevertheless, I was instantly captivated. I would follow her around the campus which I had deluded myself into thinking was harmless infatuation, but of course it was stalking – unjustifiable by any means. This was my first foray into criminal activity. Running around, hiding behind bushes, trapesing through streets became tiresome and my desire became stronger. I must make contact I thought. This depraved behaviour is futile.

I plucked up the courage to talk to her again. She was very accommodating, all most sympathetic to my 'condition', as she put it. She must be attracted to my unique brand of madness I thought. I asked her out on a date which she surprisingly agreed, under the condition that a friend could accompany her, who turned out to be a man. She claimed he was a friend, but I interpreted his presence as a fellow competitor for her affection. The floozy. We must do battle. Witty remarks and keen insights were the only weaponry needed. I must appear interesting at first, sustaining this for the duration of the relationship will be an unenviable task. By then of course I had hoped to have charmed her for long enough for love to manifest. It is a relentless pursuit with very little reward, but I must have her and embrace the tender moments. Ah yes, tempestuous love was the nature of this relationship. On that particular night I excelled myself, running amok of my opponent. She succumbed to my advances, and I invited her back to my flat to smoke cigarettes and chat. She didn't smoke at the time, but my request was not met with disapproval. Rather she inhaled the ash remedy for my sake. The precedence had been set and I felt nothing but anguish for corrupting this pristine heroine my heart so desired. How I tarnished this elegant woman with my mere presence. I gave her my bed and retired to the sofa to be tormented by my imagination.

"Are you a homosexual?" I heard her shout.

I sprang to my feet, sprinted through to the bedroom.

"May I get under the covers with you?"

"Yes, you dummy."

That night we kissed and made passionate love which came to a premature end. Despite the lack of control of my bodily functions a romance blossomed. We would have in depth discussions about many subjects, in some cases heated debates. Our main area of interest was the physiology of the human brain. I was disappointed that her ongoing education hadn't provided her with the answers I sought. My inquisition was in vain. It was a scathing indictment of the education system. This did not diminish the love I had for her. That all came some months later when she started to court another man, yes, she solicited his attention. I would know, I was there, observing. He was much larger than I, intimidated by his mere presence, I instead approached him in a passive manner seeking to diffuse the situation.

"Excuse me, excuse me. May I talk with you?"

"The creep. What do you want?"

"You're cruising for a bruising."

He swung a fist, I parried it the best I could, but he overpowered me, and I fell to the ground. I adjusted my stance and went for the knockout with my customary uppercut but my hand to eye coordination was off and I missed completely. He pushed me and I went tumbling through the air. He was either slow witted or toying with me as he gave me the opportunity to get to my feet. A last resort tact came to mind, and I kicked him with full force in the testicles. He went out with a yelp and collapsed on the ground. I turned and fled the scene. From that day there was a bounty on my head, but somehow, I avoided retaliation. I remained fearful of him despite my victory and was left with no option but to observe from afar their burgeoning relationship. I could not relinquish my possessive attitude towards her, and I shall not surrender to this dishonourable leech. The fight had provoked another strategy which was more akin to my inclination towards pacifism. I would get in my car, drive to her address and park down the street to see if she brought him home. I would causally walk the boundary of the premises, in a territorial display of dominance but of course this was a façade. Had he appeared I would have taken flight only to return more determined to intervene in his absence. I was intent on chasing shadows.

My reconnaissance had not gone unnoticed. At first, I would not acknowledge her, pretending that I was invisible, and if she spoke to me, I would say "just passing by" which was met with a frown. When she pressed me on why I was continually walking past her flat, I would say I just came by to see you. Does your boyfriend need an invitation? I would ask rhetorically, expecting her to understand, naturally she didn't. Instead, she would emphatically castigate me for my unequivocal creepy behaviour. Separation was her solution. With my heart adequately broken and my mind on the verge of psychosis, I made a conscious decision to solicit the attention, of preferably, a woman with an antithetical character and grace to distract myself. My subsequent relationships were causal and short with promiscuity being the essence. She altered my attitude to the opposite sex to an apathetic state and atypical behaviour. I was to be alone for many years. As for my current situation, I enrolled at a less illustrious university in the city, in respect of her wishes, and resigned myself to debilitating bereavement. I was a shadow of my former self and lost all motivation for associations and commitments to life.

Despite the outcome of our relationship, she had reinforced the conviction I had to establish the plausibility and application of my meanderings. I took the opportunity some years later to get back in contact with her to see if she had acquired the suitable knowledge to address some of the more pertinent questions I had. Or least this is what I told myself. I had already consulted various experts, utilising my status and connections as a professor. During these conversations I disguised my conjecture by appearing as a hapless nut on the verge of collapse rather than on a scientific breakthrough. They have most likely been confronted by this on a daily basis so were happy enough to entertain my illogical speculations. Yet I had not ascertained anything conclusive from their learning, in part, through my reluctance to divulge the finer details.

One glorious afternoon I received a phone call. It was a return call from none other than the enchantress herself, I felt I could confide in her. I had left a message on her answer machine, and she had obliged.

"Hello Ethan, how did you get my number?"

"That's not important."

"Oh dear, Ethan… I hope history is not going to repeat itself?"

"I assure you; I am not pursuing you nor do I have any interest in romantic relations with you. I have an important question to ask."

"How nice. Where shall I begin…"

"Allow me to interrupt you. Is it possible through chemical synthesis to produce brain-derived neurotrophic factor in a laboratory?"

"What? That's an inappropriate question to ask, Ethan. Are you that selfish that you don't take interest in what I have experienced in life since we last spoke?"

"Have mercy on me. Must I endure that?"

"No consideration for my feelings, you haven't changed Ethan."

"Please answer the question."

"I don't know, Ethan but if all else fails try a dead body."

"You are suggesting I extract it from a cadaver?"

"Yes, good luck with that. Goodbye Ethan."

"Wait, why are you laughing? I never considered that was possible."

She hung up the phone and that was the last I ever heard from her. It became more apparent over the year that followed that I had no choice but to extract brain-derived neurotrophic factor from the cerebral cortex and hypothalamus of a corpse, which culminated in a brief moment of salvation when I spoke to a Dr Bertrand McDougal, who claimed that he could reproduce the neurotrophins with his team but the expense he quoted me was extortionate. I had no choice but to appeal to Dr Scholtz for funding.

"Dr Scholtz, I have an associate who can reproduce the protein, in his laboratory, that is integral to my experimentation. I must further emphasise that without it I cannot proceed."

"Ah yes, the elusive protein. How much will it cost?"

I whispered the amount into Dr Scholtz ear.

"That is an obscene amount of money Dr Barrett."

"Dr Scholtz, I wouldn't ask unless it was absolutely necessary to the success of my experimentation. Surely this institute can spare the money for one of its lead researchers?"

"We set aside a budget for your project, and this was not accounted for; therefore, I must reject your request."

I almost begged but I could not forgo my dignity. Though this was a particular instance in my life where it would have been justified.

"Can you define my budget, so I know my limitations?"

"You may use the reactor as many times as you like but beyond that, you have zero funds."

"I have an alternative plan that I want you to consider."

"Go on."

"I want to extract the protein from the brain of cadavers."

"That has to be the most radical but absurd thing I've heard. Brilliant. Excuse the laugher."

"It's okay, I have become accustomed to that response."

"You're in-luck Dr Barrett. I can gain you access to the mortuary in Gartnavel General Hospital."

"Astounding, I have pondered this somewhat and would prefer the body to be frozen utilising liquid nitrogen to preserve the protein and prevent decomposition. I can't afford corruption of the organic compound. Another hinderance, is to gain permission from the donor or their kin."

"Don't concern yourself with that Dr Barrett, I am sure it won't be too exorbitant a request to accommodate the hyper-freezing of the corpses and I shall take care of the bureaucracy."

"One more thing, I am no surgeon. I would end up massacring the brain and skull. What if the donor has an open coffin?"

"They could be cremated."

"That's beside the point."

"I will have a semi-retired consultant surgeon who now occupies himself with the medical practice of pathology, to assist you."

"Assist? Dr Scholtz, I may have misled you. I think it would be best if I just observe."

"Very well."

I departed my abode and walked down the steps. When I caught sight of my Aston Martin, a smile came across my face. This was fleeting as my car had been inconsiderately wedged between two motor vehicles. I spent five minutes edging back and forth to get the car out, and subsequently, I encountered traffic. All this horsepower and no way to release it. The escalating rage against humanity was offset by the brief moments I could accelerate and experience the exceptional torque of the car. A favourable distraction, that pacified me. I rarely indulged in ostentatious displays, but I could not help but find delight in been seen in this machine of divine beauty. The interior, too, was gratifying. Some months later the novelty wore off, compounded by the sheer concentration of the nuisance. No matter what I was driving it could not alleviate my loathing and hopelessness. The traffic having subsided, with a shifting stream of consciousness, I arrived a Gartnavel General Hospital.

"Good morning, I have an appointment with Dr Archibald."

"Please take a seat, I will inform him you are here."

"Dr Barrett?"

"Yes. Good morning, Dr Archibald."

"It is but that. Please follow me."

I followed Dr Archibald into his office.

"Take a seat, Dr Barrett. I have been briefed by Dr Scholtz and met with your company's legal counsel. I have a few donors in our wards who provided written consent allowing us to perform a non-invasive procedure on the cranium and brain. The reason for this is somewhat of a mystery to not only myself but to my patients, but despite this they have agreed, in the name of research."

"That is why I am here, for the advancement of medical science... You can locate brain-derived neurotrophic factor in the patient's brain?"

"Of course, with the aid of a stereotactic frame, I will insert a biopsy needle into a burr hole and extract the protein. Simple. However, I will have to do this with multiple donors as the volume you require is substantially more than what I can expect from one patient."

"Old school."

"It's an invaluable method, Dr Barrett."

"What's the timeframe for this?"

"As a pathologist, the referral of patients to me is under condition of their prognosis which is severely bad so not too long, I would say six months."

"Great. How do we preserve the neurotrophins?"

"We will flash freeze the protein in aliquots. It will be stored with fifty percent glycerol and kept at minus twenty degrees Celsius."

"That should do it. I presume it will be delivered to my lab?"

"I will have it delivered to your lab."

I had business cards especially made for this type of shindig.

"If there are any complications to our arrangement, please keep me informed, this is the number for my work mobile."

"I hope the pharmaceutical business is treating you well?"

"It is indeed. I have one more favour to ask of you..."

"Dr Barrett, my generosity is not without limit. But please do go on…"

"I have another surgical procedure I want you to perform."

"Dr Barrett, I don't think you realise the difficulty and persuasion that is required to gain informed consent from the patient. Many people have an aversion to their body being tampered with after death unless it saves a life, and quite frankly, I don't think your cause fits into this category. I have collaborated with the legal consultant employed by your company to fabricate the paperwork in order for this research to be approved by the chief scientist office. I have committed a criminal offence. I could have my medical licence revoked, sent to prison and for what? You? The stranger of a friend. If it were not for Dr Scholtz, I would have entertained this escapade I would have exposed it to the authorities. Now divulge the truth."

"Dr Archibald, the surgery will be performed on me."

"I have to say this just got interesting."

"I want you to inject the neurotrophins into my brain… It's not a laughing matter Dr Archibald."

"I'm sorry, I just can't believe my ears. Did you say what I think you did?"

"Yes, but that is not all, it will be irradiated with gamma rays."

"Ah this just gets better."

"Stop laughing."

"I can't help it."

After some time, Dr Archibald composed himself and I could see the expression on his face change when he could see I was serious.

"That is an absurd and hysterical notion. But for that reason, I will do the procedure. I want to be a part of this through some morbid interest."

"You will?"

"Yes, and I am very familiar with the procedure, convection enhanced delivery."

"What is that?"

"It is a minimally invasive surgical exposure of the brain…"

"Exposure of the what?!"

"The brain, Dr Barrett. I will be using the methodology of a stereotactic surgery. Initially, I will make burr holes in the skull followed by the placement and feeding of small diameter catheters through the cranium and interstitial spaces, until I can reach the specific parts of the brain, the hippocampus and cortex, where I presume you want the interaction to take place. The concoction you provide me with will be delivered through the catheters using an infusion pump. Any questions?"

"And what will that effect be?"

"Most likely death, Dr Barrett."

"Sounds promising. So, you can arrange this?"

"Yes, when you are ready, I will have you scheduled into theatre and have a bed in the ward kept for your… recovery. That is if it is needed."

"Stop laughing. Are you being facetious?"

"First of all, if you survive the acute radiation syndrome it will be a miracle."

"Dr Archibald excuse the condescension but please do let me explain. Theoretically, the introduction of a high concentration of brain derived neurotrophic factor will cause neurons to grow and will contribute extensively to neuronal plasticity, changing the structure of my brain, potentially enlarging it. But combined with the gamma radiation, I have an inclination that it will supercharge these nerve cells, enhancing my mental faculties to a hyperphysical capacity. I too, have an expectation of a rare occurrence, contrary to radiotherapy, I predict that it will strengthen neural stem cells making them resistant to damage, consequently, producing glia which protect neurons. Preserving the constitution of my brain at an unprecedented development. My theory only encompasses the brain, contamination of my other organs must be prevented and since you can bypass the blood brain barrier with a surgical procedure directly injecting the substance into my brain, it will now be advantageous, preventing contamination reaching any other part of my body."

"That's quite a theory Dr Barrett... but it's complete nonsense. Do me a favour and shut the door on the way out."

"Let's get down to brass tacks, what is it going to cost? Come on give me a figure."

"You're willing to pay to kill yourself?"

I took a cigarette from the pack and light it up in his office.

"Yes, Dr Archibald."

"Put that out."

Dr Archibald wrote the sum on a piece of paper and passed it to me.

"Done."

"Okay this time I will make the arrangements. Like we agreed, I will have the brain derived neurotrophic factor sent to your office so you can expose it to radiation. Give me one weeks' notice and I will have the theatre prepped, the bed waiting, and I will even provide a dedicated private nurse. Hopefully, we can keep you alive... In the event of your death, I will have to fabricate a cause, do you object to this?"

"No, I don't mind. Thank you. Goodbye Dr Archibald."

"I look forward to receiving payment and please do keep me updated with your progress."

During the first year of training with Dr Roland Campbell I was summoned to the executive level for a meeting with Dr Scholtz. Never had I been called to his office over the public address system, he usually went out his way to visit me, hence why our friendship developed. I quickly reflected on past events to ascertain what I had done wrong. Intuition led me to believe I was about to be reprimanded and potentially fired, or worse murdered. I had my concerns even before Dr Campbell's disappearance from conversations with fellow employees, who were inclined to gossip, claiming they had been threatened with death. I procrastinated. Shuffled papers on my desk and logged onto my browser for techniques in self-defence. If I am about to go down, it will not be without a fight. A second announcement was made, and I languished my way to Dr Scholtz's office. I knocked on his door, walked away and hid around the corner of the corridor.

"Is that you Dr Barrett?"

"Oh, yes, I was just making my way to your office."

"Were you hiding?"

"Of course not, Dr Scholtz. Don't be ridiculous."

I accompanied Dr Scholtz into his office. There was a strange man seated – he had to be a hitman. I was done for. I picked up a chair and started swinging it in a frenzied attack hoping to incapacitate my enemy.

"What the hell are you doing Dr Barrett?"

"I can deduce why I am here."

"I don't think you can Dr Barrett. Put the chair down and take a seat on it."

I did as he said.

"This is Dr Patrick McAllister he is the attending physician at this laboratory. He will be performing a medical on you, this is mandatory for all staff members. Please follow him so he can do his assessment."

I followed Dr McAllister to his office. He performed an overzealous medical examination.

"Drop your trousers… bend over."

"Your quite mistaken, my name is not Ben Dover, its Ethan Barrett, I thought you were aware of that."

"Dreadful joke."

"Let me know if you find my dignity in there."

"Amusing."

"I think its polite and customary for me to get the bill."

"You're quite the comedian."

"I hope you're going to buy me flowers after that."

"Not likely, anyway. Please take this medication. You will be administered it on your arrival at this facility which will be followed by a one hour extended break from seven thirty am to eight thirty am when work will commence."

"What's the diagnosis Doc?"

"Nothing to be concerned about. It's a company's policy to ensure that the employees are docile, calm and obedient."

"So, you want to control me?"

"Of course not, Dr Barrett. This is a treatment to improve your wellbeing."

"Since it's a company policy… is it prescribed to all employees?"

"Yes, Dr Barrett. Its mandatory."

I strongly objected and remonstrated with Dr McAllister, but he would not concede. He stressed that my employment would be terminated immediately if I did not take the medication. I went straight to Dr Scholtz's office where I was reprimanded for my insubordination and addressed as a fool for not following the physician's recommendation.

"But its mandatory for everyone!" I pleaded. "Surely all of the employees can't have the same diagnosis?"

"I suppose we should call the ailment the human condition."

"You're joking right?"

"Not at all. Dr Barrett we have had a certain amount of camaraderie between the two of us. I regard you as a friend, and I too hope you hold me in the same esteem. Giving this friendship can you not trust my judgement? If not, that of a qualified physician?"

"I think what you are asking me is disproportionate to our level of trust."

"Just take the medication Dr Barrett it will improve your wellbeing."

"That's quite a claim, one shared only with Dr McAllister. If you allow me to continue my experimentation without interference, my welfare would be at maximum capacity."

"This matter is not open for discussion. Please return to Dr McAllister's office to be administered your first dosage."

"I want you to acknowledge my indignation at your decision. I should quit out of principle, let alone for being coerced into taking an unknown drug."

"The identity of the medication may be unknown to you at this current juncture, but it has been proven to improve happiness and productivity resulting in an increase in prosperity. Does this not sound appealing to you?"

"Is this a new approach?"

"The pills or termination, Dr Barrett. Your future is in your hands."

I was irate. I stormed out of Dr Scholtz office. Flouncing along like a man possessed, I made my way to Dr McAllister's office to swallow the mystery capsule.

"Dr McAllister, before this dissolves in my gut... What's the damage?"

"Slim to none. Just relax."

I was starting to perspire; I had no inclination what was about to happen to me. I had been involuntarily exposed to another conspiracy within this nefarious corporation. The portrayal of these obvious clinical trials as a benevolent intervention for betterment of the personnel may have misled some but my suspicions would not allow me to be deceived. This was a calculated and covert endeavour to maintain ownership and a patent until their experimental drug was either licenced by the appropriate government department, the medicines and healthcare products regulatory agency, or was prohibited under the jurisdiction of the misuse of drugs act, thus falling within the category of a controlled substance. The latter would be a financial pitfall hence why they are conducting their research in house as opposed to throwing money at clinical studies. They had proven themselves to be shrewd entrepreneurs and conniving evil masterminds, and who was at the heart of this industry, my good friend Dr Scholtz. He had resorted to extreme lengths to keep this from leaking out and gaining publicity. I presume he identified the weakness of all employees, as he had done with me to gain leverage, enabling him to supress any potential informants. This was an assault on the civil rights of those accredited with their success and development solely for the purpose of exploitation and profiteering. The carefully orchestrated induction interlaced with bribery was one of many phases of control. The pinnacle of this suppression was a drug causing susceptibility to their conditioning; desensitising and coercing us to affiliate ourselves with their insidious scheme in order to promote our own prosperity and wellbeing.

My weakness was an absence of prospects to achieve the objective of my research. In the healthcare system there is a comparable technique to treat cancer to the experimentation I deem to conduct, and given to any form of insanity, I expect a different result. I could have surreptitiously gained access to an external radiotherapy machine through acquiring the appropriate qualifications in the medical profession, and when in solitary, aimed the external ionizing radiation at the neurotrophins. What inhibited me from spending many years of my life at medical school for the sole purpose of infiltrating a Cobalt unit, is that they are not widely accessible, and only 1 MeV of energy is produced from the decay of irradiated Cobalt metal, which is inadequate. The apparent alternative is to gain employment at the only nuclear reactor in the nation. Job vacancies are rarity at this facility and despite my credentials I would probably be overlooked from someone who is more suitably qualified given my theoretical background.

The last resort would be to infiltrate what is considered to be the most protected private facility in the nation. Three concentric circles of security measures becoming increasingly more impenetrable the closer in proximity one gets.

Relatively lax is the 'owner-controlled area' which is merely sign posted to prevent anyone from trespassing. This I could bypass with ease. The next stage dubbed the 'protected area' has somewhat more sophisticated countermeasures. The anti-climb barbed wired fences could be overcome easily with wire cutters. I could evade the security cameras by shining an infra-red light directly into the lens obscuring my appearance and concealing my identity. As for the civil nuclear constabulary, given my lack of experience in combat I would have to neutralise them with a tranquilizer gun, incapacitating them with a heavy sedative. I would procure this weaponry by breaking into a veterinary hospital. Having circumvented the exterior fortification, I am confronted by locked and alarmed security doors which contain the 'vital area' where the reactor is situated. I lack the expertise to override the locking system so I would have to commandeer parts off the black market and assemble a bomb at home, attach the explosive and blow it open; of course, this would attract a lot of attention so would have to create a decoy by having a simultaneous explosion somewhere else in the power plant. From there I would take out whatever guards I come across with my tranquiliser. Gain access to the core, insert the neurotrophins and eureka.

I sat on Dr McAllister's couch waiting for some sort of manifestation in sensation, I began to ruminate further on which future scenario would be the most achievable. With a shifting stream of consciousness, I began to chuckle. These dastardly schemes were too ludicrous to consider any further. I had to confront reality and admit that I am truly indebted to this organisation. I became increasingly uncomfortable with my current predicament. I looked over at Dr McAllister who seemed to have ignored the laughter and continued to type on his computer keyboard. A sinister compulsion came over me. I walked over to the cabinet picked up an ornament, walked over to Dr McAllister, held it above his head, with the intention of smashing it against his skull. Suddenly, it hit, I dissolved.

Chapter 2
Biological Phenomenon

Recurrence of the tormented morning that frequently confronted me, had me disturbed; and in concurrence with the adversaries on the tarmac, in my sub-conscious, and oppressive withdrawals; I was exasperated by the time it came to swallow that capsule. I got in line at my designated dispensary which was one of many in the facility. I lingered by the door like a fiend anticipating a fix, becoming more agitated as time passed. I began to pace. At last Dr McAllister opened his door and the hapless addicts began to shuffle into an orderly queue, a few disgruntled tussles broke out but mostly they were courteous despite the severity of the inconvenience. My turn soon approached, and I gobbled the pill down without reprehension. Impatiently, I awaited the absorption of the tablet in my bloodstream to appease my craving, which was fulfilment at its lowest form, what was a greater affection was the acute sensation of euphoria that contrasts the dark and sinister hallucinations, which had become more frequent with every dosage I took. It was paradoxical to see these horrors but to feel unbound joy at their perception. Astonishingly, I was being unwillingly rehabilitated into a psychotic sadist and I had nothing but enthusiasm for the process. I could not believe this was mandatory and began to condone the practice to others. It was far superior to a hit of caffeine and nicotine that the drones have become accustomed to. Dr McAllister joked that it prevented them incurring costs for employees signing off with mental related illnesses. "It's therapy in a pill." He would say. Thirty minutes later when the effect had died down, I was ready to make up for the unproductive start to the day.

Lunch was soon upon me, and I made my way to the cafeteria. I had organised to meet Dr Harp, who I was on better terms with, and a Dr Dunbar and Dr Dougal, newcomers to the social melee.

"How was the mood-altering phenomenon this morning, Dr Harp?"

"For what reason is it a phenomenon, Dr Barrett?"

"Why because there are no negative physiological aftereffects, apart from a harrowing craving that returns with bitter vengeance in the morning."

"You mean, there is no come down."

"You seem well adapted to the drug culture, Dr Harp, but yes. It seems illogical. The flooding of the brain with neurotransmitters could only cause a depletion leaving the brain destitute of serotonin, resulting in severe depression and yet I feel no difference. It's as if it didn't happen."

"It is quite miraculous in that respect but lest we forget it is simply an amphetamine derivative."

"It shares one quality with the drug you are referring to, Dr Harp. An elevated mood to the extent of euphoria but that's where the comparison ends, and Dr Barrett, there is no addictive properties inherent in the pharmaceutical, perhaps the absence of positive stimuli is causing your symptoms.

This an acute antidepressant, it's not a party drug with all the associated druggie effects. It's akin to a selective serotonin reuptake inhibitor, stimulating production of the hormone dopamine and inhibiting absorption of serotonin by the nerve cell, but not to the extent to deprive the brain; hence why depression is not an associated side effect."

"Interesting Dr Dunbar. I feel less guilty about taking it, even if I am obligated to."

"Dr Dunbar is a pharmaceutical technician. He is instrumental in the development of this mysterious wonder drug that has us all talking."

"Bravo, Dr Dunbar."

"You mentioned the physical aftereffects but what about the psychological, Dr Barrett? Do you care to confide in us?"

"No such problems to share."

"I will…"

"Go ahead, Dr Dougal."

"I hide in my closet as I feel a greater presence than my own."

"I have a similar experience, Dr Dougal, but in my dreams, I soon dismiss it."

"Your both nuts, no wonder their giving you pills."

"And you, Dr Harp, are you the epitome of sanity?"

"Certainly am."

"I have to confess that I am having hallucinations."

"It's not uncommon, Dr Barrett with a selective serotonin reuptake inhibitor but you are the first reported case with this particular variant. I will schedule you an appointment with myself and Dr McAllister to discuss. But in the meantime, my opinion of the cause is most likely related to…"

"Forget that Dr Dunbar. What do you see Dr Barrett?"

"Today I saw a dead, desolate planet with human bodies scattered about with their rotting flesh being devoured by maggots. There was a dying tree on the horizon wrapped in barbed wire, it was bleeding and seemed as if it was gasping for air, but I felt nothing but pure joy at the sight."

"That's shocking. Truly shocking, Dr Barrett."

"Why did you roll your eyes and shake your head? Are you desensitised to horror?"

"Excuse the laughter… But I must not be getting the right pills… Or perhaps…?"

"What Dr Harp?"

"My dose might not be high enough… Excuse me, gentleman. I have a meeting I must attend."

"I do wonder what other affects it has on my brain."

"Studies have shown that users who stop taking ecstasy have a marked decrease in brain activity in such regions as the amygdala and hippocampus."

"So, it impedes learning, stunts the memory and hinders emotional processing."

"That's an accurate description, Dr Barrett."

"This may be a psychoactive medication, gentleman, but it's not a street drug mixed with all those adulterants. But more conclusively, there is an absence of toxicity in monkeys, in other words, no associated damaging effects, and so far, it has been a reliable predictor."

"Wasn't much of tangent, Dr Dunbar. I will interject with the following… Animals have rights! And to the matter at hand, your attitude is reminiscent of Dr McAllister. Is it mandatory for you to take the 'medication', as you put it?"

"I am not exempt."

"I have yet to find an exception to the rule, Dr Dunbar. What steps did you take to prepare, Dr Dougal?"

"I compiled a mixed playlist of Avant-garde jazz which in retrospect was not a good idea. The obscure and disorganised phrases soon confused me, and I ran to hid in my closet."

"You must spend a lot of time in there, Dr Dougal?"

"He is getting accustomed to the pills."

"Is that right Dr Dunbar? I bought a reclining chair for my office – very comfortable. Perfect for the occasion. I seem to persevere irrespective of any dilemma, which is comforting."

"You mean you've become absent-minded, Dr Barrett."

"I suppose I have, Dr Dunbar."

"On that note I must go. Goodbye, Dr Barrett. Goodbye Dr Dougal."

I sat and spoke with Dr Dougal about the eerie experiences but after a while the conversation became relatively mundane in comparison to the very thing we were discussing. Yes, the extraordinary pills were far more compelling than any argument against it. I had finally become servile, a fully-fledged addict. In whatever degree of rational I had left led me to believe I had an addictive personality.

"You do realise that we are merely test subjects; lab rats if you will. Our utility is marginalised, surpassed by a commodity. It's hard to comprehend how unethical this practice is."

"This is nothing compared to their nuclear programme."

"What nuclear programme?"

"I thought everyone knew within the organisation?"

"Is there something you're not telling me?"

"Wait, what's your position again?"

"I am laboratory analyst."

"Brilliant. This is classified information I'm about to impart..."

"Do go on."

"On second thought you don't have clearance... Ah, I'm just winding you up about the nuclear programme. Anyway... at first I was forced to take the pill but now I do it through choice."

"Keep telling yourself that, Dr Barrett."

"I evaluated the administering of this unknown substance as a mandatory condition of employment. And concluded, that it was worth taking it given the opportunity they presented me with. How could I refuse. The withdrawals are negligible in consideration of the reward, and I have been reassured numerous times that it is harmless, but more importantly, I'm happy for the first time in a long time."

"That happiness is artificial. They are trying to control us and brainwash us."

"It's certainly more effective than subliminal messages and propaganda."

"Are you that far gone?"

"Why are you so reluctant Dr Dougal?"

"Because it's a dangerous drug."

"Let's agree to disagree. I don't consider anything unethical about it."

"You're a druggie."

"I dare say you've been brainwashed by societal moral standards. Are you not an advocate of cultural relativism? Perhaps you need another dose of nihilism."

"You're the patron saint of cruel."

"Sure... whatever you say."

Dr Dougal got up and stormed off.

"That's right have your tantrum elsewhere, you child."

I strolled to my office through the ecological garden in the centre of the campus. Very peaceful.

"Put that out."

"Excuse my misconduct good Sir."

I extinguished my cigarette and sauntered on. I thought of how acrimonious that exchange had become. I considered regressing to the life of a recluse. These social gatherings did not appeal to me.

"Dr Barrett, over here."

"Hello, Dr Harp. Before you say anything, I have a concern. I may have told Dr Dougal about the nuclear programme."

"No need to be concerned. I will have a chat with him."

"Great. Why did you call me over?"

"Look what I have."

"Your key card?"

"It's not mine, its Dr McAllister's key card."

"How did you get that?"

"The old switcheroo."

"Fascinating, I have work to attend to speak later."

"No Dr Barrett, I need a lookout. Come with me."

We walked to Dr McAllister's office where Dr Harp opened his door with the key card. I was told to stand outside and make sure no one notices. After some time, Dr Harp came out with a plastic bag, it seemed to have something in it. I followed Dr Harp back to his office.

"What's in the bag?"

"The mystery pills, Dr Barrett. Now we don't have to wait, and I can increase my dosage to have my own superior enlightening visions."

"Give me one."

"That's all you take. You're a lightweight."

I swallowed the pill, excused myself and made my way to my office. Already an accomplice, I didn't want to be implicated by the loot. I must distance myself from this depraved act, it is the only scenario in which I can deny my involvement. Despite my trials and tribulations, once a day was enough for me. I was concerned that Dr Harp might overdose but I made no attempt to stage an intervention.

I was now twenty-nine years old, having spent eight years of my life at university attaining my PhD and one-year lecturing. My career at this institution having spanned over two years. A yearlong tutelage by Dr Roland Campbell. My own autodidact period of learning the operation and familiarisation of the nuances of the reactor lasted a year. On the completion of my apprenticeship, I anxiously waited for brain-derived neurotrophic factor to be delivered, which I think contributed to my addiction to the psychedelic antidepressant, that they were periodically, and generously I may add, dosing us with. Dr Archibald did not renege on his word but was far from punctual – one year to be exact. Upon delivery of the extracted protein, I was walking through the corridor on my way to my office, with a small portable freezer box. An announcement was made over the public address system, but I was too engrossed in my experiment to take notice of it. I heard loud footsteps coming from behind me which caught my attention, they were getting closer, and it seemed as if the gait was getting longer. Whoever it was they were galloping at some rate. I stepped to the side to let them by shielding the freezer box to prevent any calamity.

"Dr Barrett! Dr Barrett. We've been foiled!"

"I don't have time for this Dr Harp."

"We need to get our story straight."

"Dr Harp and Dr Barrett, please report to Dr Scholtz's office."

"Did you implicate me?"

"I threw you under the bus Dr Barrett."

"Did they offer you immunity in return for your testimony?"

"Yes, Dr Barrett. I am the primary witness."

"You swine. Now I have to rectify your devious behaviour and clear my name."

"Not if I have anything to do with it."

"I think it's appropriate in this situation to underestimate you, Dr Harp."

Off I went to Dr Scholtz's office with Dr Harp to prove my innocence. As I walked into the room, I noticed Dr Scholtz temperament was expressed legibly on his face.

"How do you plead, Dr Barrett?"

"Not guilty."

"This would be the time to confess."

I proceeded to outline the events that took place much to Dr Harp's consternation.

"That contradicts Dr Harp's portrayal. He said that you blackmailed him into stealing the pharmaceutical drugs."

"With what leverage?"

"Good question Dr Barrett. Do you care to address this Dr Harp?"

"He said if I didn't do it, he would blame me for the entire ploy."

"That's your excuse? Nonsense. I am telling you the truth Dr Scholtz. It was that conniving degenerate."

"Your clearly unaware that there are security cameras in our pharmacies. It caught Dr Harp in the act. Yet you are nowhere to be seen Dr Barrett. In fact, your last known whereabouts was in the garden having a conversation with none other than Dr Harp. Were you threatening him?"

"Absolutely not. He asked me to be a lookout whilst he stole the drugs."

"Dr McAllister your employment has been terminated. Security will escort you to your office where you can gather your possessions. Thereafter, I will go through the non-disclosure agreement with you with the purpose of emphasizing the repercussions."

"What just cause do you have to fire me?"

"You flatter to deceive, Dr Harp."

"Silence, Dr Barrett. He is the one who is guilty of this larceny."

"That's enough Dr Harp. You are dismissed."

Dr Harp's face turned a shade of green, he got to his feet, stumbled out the room. Still audible, I heard him vomit and collapse on the floor. I rushed out to the corridor to ascertain his well-being. Security was lifting him to his feet and began to drag him off to I presume his office. Dr Scholtz joined me in the corridor.

"I will have the cleaners attend to the mess, but back to the matter at hand. I found Dr McAllister's key card and the medication in Dr Harp's office. This gives me reason to doubt that this was your scheme, and had you planted them there then well that's beyond my comprehension."

"I am glad justice has prevailed."

"You are not absolved quite yet Dr Barrett. I'm giving you a verbal warning and you are now on probation. If there is one more misdemeanour, I will fire you on the spot."

"Understood."

"I intend to purge this organisation of reprobates who may bring this company into disrepute. Please accompany me to Dr Harp's office."

"I don't think I have the stomach for that, Dr Scholtz."

Security was barring entry into Dr Harp's office. They stepped aside for Dr Scholtz. The security guards had restrained Dr Harp with zip ties, he was lying motionless on the floor – he must have resisted. Dr Scholtz approached him and injected a substance into his arm.

"I can't risk a potential informant, Dr Barrett, jeopardizing all the important work we have been doing here. The board have permitted me to use lethal force to prevent a leak."

"That's ironic… And for you to arbitrate the sentence and enforce the punishment that has come as a complete surprise, Dr Scholtz."

"As CEO, I have a responsibility to my employers… They have, however, paid me handsomely to renounce ethics."

"I am not sure I could put a sum on that, Dr Scholtz."

"You will in time Dr Barrett. No matter our intentions at some stage we will disregard our moral principles for a vice far more fulfilling, it's inevitable."

"You seem to think you know me better than I know myself."

"I am a good judge of character, Dr Barrett."

"You take me for a murder?"

"Perhaps with a little persuasion."

Whilst he was convulsing on the floor, I searched the room with my eyes looking for a suitable exit, but none could be discovered. After an excruciatingly long time he lay still.

"Check his pulse, Dr Barrett."

Morbid curiosity compelled me to check, I knew he was dead.

"I feel no pulse, Dr Scholtz... How do you plan to dispose of the body?"

Dr Scholtz pulled out a folded body bag from his suitcase.

"We put him in this, Dr Barrett, courtesy of the gullible Dr Archibald. Wait here. Okay gentleman, he is willing to cooperate, we can take it from here. Your dismissed."

The security guards left without witnessing the gruesome crime. I stood in silence with a serial killer and his latest victim, fully aware that the knowledge I now possess was of far greater value than my life. Having sealed Dr Harp in the body bag Dr Scholtz left the room without any notice. I was concerned he would return with the authorities and accuse me of the murder, but he returned alone with a trolly covered with a blanket.

"It's quite convenient you're here, spare my back for once. Please help me lift him onto the trolley."

I did as he said. We wheeled the body out to a car, placed him into the boot and drove off. I was paranoid that we would be apprehended by the police for some unrelated charge, such as a broken taillight, leading to the discovery of the body. Dr Scholtz spoke about his retirement plans as we drove through the countryside. He was unaffected and nonchalant about the whole situation. Clearly a pro. He pulled into a forest, took out a bag of lime and a couple of shovels.

"You will assist me in digging a hole, then we will spread lime to prevent the stench of decomposition. We must go deep into the forest. You take the head for the sake of my back."

"Dr Scholtz, are you aware of the rumours within the organisation? They suspect a murderer."

"Yes, that was a diversionary tactic. I had an emissary threaten a few employees with death if they did not comply with his instructions and spread rumours that the sudden disappearance of staff was due to murder. The gossip surrounding this escapade escalated to the point that it defied reason to believe, or so I've been told."

"That's throwing caution to the wind."

"Despite the impression I may have given, I took no pleasure in killing Dr Harp, it was a duty, but I am not immune to the thrill of being on the precipice of condemnation."

"You have different desires to me."

"Besides, I am not concerned. The non-disclosure agreement will prevent anything transpiring to the public domain. Think about it, does anyone out with the organisation know you are employed by me?"

"Only Dr Wilde."

"And that was my first mistake. Get in the hole Dr Barrett."

"Please don't kill me, Dr Scholtz."

"What do you take me for an executioner?"

"Well yes. I can't think of a more appropriate name."

"Just spread the lime."

"I believed the rumours, Dr Scholtz."

"You're making this difficult for me Dr Barrett."

We filled in the hole, covered it with sticks, moss and grass, by the time we had finished the burial was completely hidden. We checked the parameter for witnesses – there were none. Whilst on the drive back to the laboratory, Dr Scholtz pulled into a layby.

"Dr Barrett, there is no honour in being a snitch, and no benefit gained. You will be portrayed as a rat within the organisation and your employment terminated as a result with a damning reference to any future employer limiting your career options. Reducing you to a worthless blight upon society. That is if I don't take matters into my own hands and despatch of you in the same manner as our dear friend Dr Harp."

"You have my word; I won't mention a thing. I am impressed, you're a pro, despite your inclination to put yourself into a vulnerable position."

"They will never suspect me, and if they do, I will condemn them to the grave."

"I have to ask... how many bodies are in that forest?"

"Some questions are best left unanswered, Dr Barrett."

I refused to be subjected to another homicide debacle. As a precaution, I alienated myself from my colleagues for the three weeks prior to my scheduled rendezvous with the reactor. In the intermittent period, I sought the necessary ingredients for my compound. The crucial component is an oxidized form of pure nicotinamide adenine dinucleotide, which after an inquisition, a capital incentive, and a notarised document of proof of no resale, I procured from a biotech company. I purchased, of my own money, one kilogram, which was produced through chemical synthesis, at a cost of four thousand five hundred pounds. A normal dosage on experimental mice is two thousand milligram per kilogram of weight thus a sufficient dosage for my stature would be one hundred and sixty-five grams. The inclusion of this molecule in my compound is due to it being a precursor to an increase of concentrations of an advantageous enzyme – by inhibiting the binding of a detrimental protein – which should theoretically, protect and counteract any damage or breaks caused to the DNA within my cells from the exposure to radiation.

On the morning of the reactor experiment I took the brain derived neurotrophic factor from the freezer, preserved by the temperature but unfrozen due to the glycerol, and added the final components, NAD+ in the form of an amorphous soluble powder, five thousand milligrams of a potassium supplement, dissolved in deionized water and a glucose syrup. I dubbed the compound Progenicepathy. I delegated the hazardous task to Stevie to affix the glass vile to the reactor. Fixed within the vile was a rod of lead approximately five centimetres in width and length. Dr Gage will intravenously inject me with a chelating agent to counteract any potential lead poisoning, during my recovery. Given the density and large quantity of electrons in the lead, its purpose is to attenuate high energy gamma rays by the means of the Compton effect, which is essentially the collision of a photon with an electron. The gamma photon and electron are not destroyed but are scattered, sharing the initial energy. The photon propagates through the lead maintaining energy until interacting with another electron, thereby ionising further atoms. Whilst the electron, set in motion, undergoes the Bremsstrahlung effect, decelerating through interaction with an atomic nucleus, whereby its kinetic energy is converted into a high energy x-ray photon. The combination of the two will irradiate the lead. The absorption rate of the gamma rays in the lead rod is equal to one joule per kilogram of matter. The weight of lead for five cubic centimetres is roughly two kilograms. Resulting in one hundred and three trillion Gray being absorbed.

148,838,400,000,000 joules / 1.45 kg = roughly 1 trillion Gray.

That accounts for absorbed radiation. To calculate the equivalent deposition of radiation from Progenicepathy in my brain tissue is quite simple since one Gray of gamma radiation has one Sievert of biological effect. A lethal dose of five Sieverts, the unit measure of how much radiation is absorbed by human tissue, is enough to kill a human being within a month of exposure.

The radiation epidemiology of Progenicepathy can be categorised as the stochastic effect, the radiation will have an indirect effect on my chromosomes, causing radiolysis to the water molecules in my brain cells, producing ions and hydroxyl radicals which aggressively bond with the DNA molecule causing structural damage, and a potential mutation. Less frequently, the radiation may directly hit the DNA causing a molecular disruption by breaking the base pairs. The ideal scenario would be that I incur sublethal injury, whereby the chromosomes are repaired correctly. The mediation of this process may be intensified with the countermeasure of high concentrations of NAD+ circulating my brain. If the brain barrier is crossed, I could develop acute radiation syndrome, a deterministic effect, which is the result of the gastrointestinal tract being highly sensitive to radiation. Dr Gage will be intravenously administering Cyclizine, in an attempt to curtail any vomiting – to be killed by dehydration as opposed to radiation would be a hard pill to swallow.

Having circumvented the negative effects on my health, I now address the beneficial phenomenon, which is underpinned by radiation hormesis, an adaptive-dose response model which claims that ionizing radiation may have a positive effect on a biological system at lower doses but detrimental at higher doses. In support of this hypothesis, I will appeal to naturally occurring exposure such as ^{40}Potassium, a radioactive isotope, that is the predominant radionuclide present within a human's body. What is relative is that five thousand ^{40}Potassium atoms undergo radioactive decay each second of which ten percent emit gamma rays, resulting in five hundred gamma rays produced each second. Some of which are attenuated in the body while others escape entirely. Radionuclides present in the body are one tenth of the natural background radiation we are exposed to. We are exposed to approximately three millisievert per year of radiation from environmental and cosmic radioactivity. We have developed a tolerance to radiation as it is a critical environmental cue for certain biological processes, in particular the immune system, by stimulating production of Lymphocytes, the white blood T cells, that destroy radiation sensitive T repressor cells, encouraging more efficiency, effectively curing cancer. If the body were deprived of radiation, homeostasis of the body would be disrupted causing physiologically stress. A study, on a radiation resistant and susceptible bacterium, conducted under ground in a vault demonstrated that the absence of radiation caused an inhibiting of growth, which returned to normal with the introduction of a naturally occurring dose of radiation. Albeit, this was bacteria, I insist it corroborates my theory. I firmly believe that Progenicepathy will transcend the inadequate naturally occurring radiation assuming the role of a radiopharmaceutical with the properties of a therapeutic agent, the presence of which is an impediment to the deterioration of the brain through neurological diseases, and simultaneously act as a growth medium that will enlarge parts of my brain exponentially, augmenting neuroplasticity, stimulating, and enhancing it beyond comprehension.

I could not return home to the futility of studying my prized collection of captivating literature in my bookshelf, nor the lazy habitual distraction of a banal television programme, followed by lying prostrate on the bed, in the grips of insomnia, staring at the roof, repressing any notion of what is about to transpire in the next seventeen hours. Instead, I tread a hole in my office carpet, transfixed on the wooden box containing the Progenicepathy concoction, the anticipation had me anguished, but I need not worry about my present health given the twenty-gauge lead lining. I sought to alleviate myself from the self-inflicted suffering by incorporating denial into my thought patterns, but despite my best efforts I was on the precipice of a mental breakdown. I was about to commit suicide, never had this course of action manifested through experience, despite any misfortune or how sorrowful I may have been. At the very least, aided by general anaesthetic, it would be painless euthanasia. I am naïve in my intentions, subscribing to transhumanism is fairly innocuous in moderation, but I must be mentally deranged to adopt an extremist agenda and endanger my life for the advancement of the physiology of the brain. I knew one means in which to negate my defective judgement and disassociate myself from the reality of the situation.

"Dr Scholtz excuse my intrusion. I'm enquiring if you can grant my request."

"Ah yes, do come in Dr Barrett, the culmination of your experimentation is within your grasp. The fleeting glimpse that is life unfolding before your eyes. You are very brave to flaunt death for a hypothesis that our species could well be improved by radiation no less."

"What's with the sarcasm?"

"I do apologise it's been a long day. Now what was it you wanted?"

"The 'medication' Dr Scholz, something to take the edge off."

"Very good, Dr Barrett I think I would resort to escapism when confronted by one's own mortality. Let's take a walk to Dr McAllister's office, he is usually around after close of business hours, perhaps he can assist."

"Thank you."

"After you Dr Barrett."

"How is Elaine?"

"The old ball and chain is well. I'm growing tired of her perspective that I am at fault for what is wrong in the world."

"Having seen you in action Dr Scholtz. I would have to agree."

"Very amusing, Dr Barrett. Here we are, and we are in luck. Good evening, Dr McAllister. Dr Barrett is in need of a cure for his pre-op nerves."

"You're having an operation Dr Barrett?"

"Just minor surgery. The usual please bar keep."

"Coming right up."

I swallowed the pill with gusto. We spoke about trivial matters for quarter of an hour as I gradually edged towards the door.

"I must be on my way, gentleman."

"I will see you tomorrow in your office Dr Barrett so I can escort you to the hospital."

"I think my sense of humour has failed me. You want to take me to the hospital?"

"Of course, I want to protect my investment. I will be observing the entire operation."

"I will be bluntly honest, given my mental fatigue after hours of rumination, I must resign myself to your arrangements and oblige to meet you in my office without argument. Goodbye."

I ran to my office so I could enjoy psychoactive experience in solitude.

"Good morning, Dr Barrett. How was the sleep?"

"What time is it?"

"It's ten am, were late, get you stuff together."

"I have a vague recollection of what happened last night?"

"Ah, Dr McAllister gave you a very powerful tranquilliser to ease you to sleep."

"You could have given me fore warning."

"Never mind that now Dr Barrett. Your about to find out on what side of the line you occupy."

"Between insanity and genius?"

"Precisely. Now let's go."

Dr Scholtz had inspired me to action, we got in the car and set off to Gartnavel hospital. Dr Scholtz announced our arrival at reception, where we were escorted to my private room in the ward. I was told to strip and adorn the attire appropriate for the occasion – a hospital gown. A gurney was brought in, and I was transported to the theatre room.

"Good morning, Dr Barrett. For the sake of brevity, we will skip over the pleasantries and get straight to the action. Where is the... how did he refer to it?"

"Progenicepathy... It's in this wooden box, Dr Archibald."

"Excellent Dr Scholtz. Once we have the frame mounted, and I have made a small, trephined hole in the skull. I want all non-essential personnel to leave the room. Dr Scholtz you may want to leave to prevent exposure."

"I'll take my chances."

"Dr Barrett, this is Dr Cuthbert, our anaesthetist."

"Hello Dr Barrett, everything will be fine, you're in safe hands."

"That's reassuring."

"Now Dr Barrett, I want you to count down from ten."

"I object to the last words coming out of my mouth to be a countdown, but so be it. Ten, nine, eight, seven, six, five..."

Chapter 3
Hyperphysical

"Hello, Ethan, awake from your sleep you fool, I, the endogenous malignancy, will flourish at your expense... Wake up, Dr Barrett!"

"This better be good, I was having the most wonderful dream."

I became conscious of my surroundings, to my relief it was familiar, but I could not locate the source of the voice. I roused myself from the couch and sat upright.

"Who said that? Reveal yourself."

I noticed that a corner of my living room was completely dark. Barely perceptible something began to move. It appeared from the shadow.

"You have caused an imbalance to the natural order."

From the very clothes on his back to the mannerism by which he spoke it was I. I stood there dumbfounded, staring at the doppelgänger. It appeared as if he was waiting for me to comprehend and address the confrontation.

"I warn you don't take one more step towards me. I will have to defend myself by any means necessary."

"I am here to restore that balance."

He charged at me, I swung a fist and connected onto his jaw, he didn't even flinch.

"Oh dear, you're as tough as nails... Erm, give me a chance to explain... that was an accident I slipped and inadvertently used your head to regain my balance."

He hesitated to ponder the excuse but then proceeded with one hand to take me by the throat and lift me off the ground.

"All most had you convinced."

He applied more pressure damn near pulverising my bones.

"His heart rate is elevated."

The imposter began to convulse violently, he dropped me to the floor. In disbelief I witnessed him split into a duplicate, it reminded me of cell mitosis. They stood motionless, fixated on me, until they spoke in unison.

"Exterminate, restore the balance."

Aggressively, they surged at me, pinned me to the ground and began to beat me to a bloody pulp. A compelling force caused them to withdraw and divide, again and again until they took up most of the living room. They did not cease in their division, soon I was compressed against the wall, by the sheer number of copies. Claustrophobia set in and I gasped for air. The pressure became unbearable, I was being crushed to death.

"He is going into cardiac arrest. I will start cardiopulmonary resuscitation, Racheal, summon the cardiac arrest team, I need a defibrillator in here."

I felt a sudden rush of an electric current through my body.

"Clear."

In an instant I regained consciousness, the pain was excruciating, I tried to muster the energy to scream in agony but all that transpired was a gentle mumble. I had what seemed like a tube in my throat. I opened my eyes, but the piercing light burned a hole in my retina. I gradually allowed my eyes to adjust, but my peripheral vision was cloudy and blurred. To get a better look at my surroundings I consciously attempted to move my head, no matter the effort it would not cooperate, and I realised I was affected by paralysis. The pain in my head was so serve that I passed out. I came to, and was disorientated, but the reassuring environment I found myself in seemed to be a hospital from all the chatter.

"Oh my god, he's stable and his eyes are open. Racheal, Racheal quickly phone Dr Archibald."

"Dr Barrett, it's me Dr Archibald. Can you move? You have been in a coma for the past four weeks on life support."

"Dr Archibald he could be in a vegetative state."

"Please refrain from stating the obvious Rachael. Dr Barrett if you can hear me blink twice."

I blinked twice.

"He could be minimally conscious, Dr Archibald."

"For goodness' sake Racheal, please allow me to handle this."

"Dr Barrett, I don't believe your consciousness is impaired, but I do wonder if you are in pain at all. Blink twice if you are in pain. Okay, Rachael get the morphine."

I felt a warm sensation wash over me and the pain disappear. I drifted off to sleep. I awoke to the sound of Dr Archibald's voice.

"Dr Barrett, let me first begin by saying what an absolute nightmare it has been to keep you alive. I had to perform a craniectomy to relieve the pressure of the inflammation of your brain. Amongst other complications, you have erythema all over your head and you have developed cataracts, all a result of exposure. Remarkably all the damage appears to have been contained to the cranium region. Rest for now Dr Barrett, in the knowledge that you have a dedicated nurse monitoring your recovery. I am not a religious man, but if by some miracle, you regain your motor functions, we will talk then."

For an unknown duration of time, my only means of communication was blinking but I was making progress. The mumbling had progressed into a discernible word.

"Help."

I would repeat this over and over whilst I lay confined to the bed.

"We are trying to help you the best we can. Dr Archibald should be here shortly. In fact, here he is now."

"How is he progressing?"

"He is able to say the word 'help', but he keeps repeating it. He may have brain damage."

"Rachael, that's an insensitive thing to say in the presence of a patient. Let's talk outside and you can express your opinion freely."

Sometime later.

"Dr Barrett, the ophthalmologist, Dr Hamilton, objected at first to performing eye surgery on a patient in the recovery stage of a coma, but I persuaded her in the end. I have scheduled you in. You will see again, Dr Barrett."

The surgery was a success, thanks to the artificial lenses I could see better than I ever had. An ointment they were rubbing onto my bald head cleared up my irritating skin condition although I had a nasty scar. Despite the effectiveness of each treatment, speech eluded me. I had a daily routine of teaching myself how to talk. Persistence gave its just reward; I eventually began to form sentences and articulate what I had intended to express.

"Dr Barrett, how are you today?"

"In some discomfort but the pain has subsided."

"Excellent. This is Miss Mackenzie. She is our resident physiotherapist. She is crucial for your next step of rehabilitation; she will implement a treatment plan to restore your functionality and movement. We will have you walking again my boy."

During one of the exercising sessions with the physiotherapist, Dr Scholtz walked in. This was the first time I saw him since the operation.

"Wonderful, your still alive Dr Barrett…"

"Alive and kicking, thanks to Miss Mackenzie."

"Do you mind giving us some privacy Miss Mackenzie?"

"Yes, of course."

"Now that we are alone Dr Barrett, I must ask, do you notice anything different? Any enhancements to speak of?"

"Nothing to report, the experiment is a resounding failure, Dr Scholtz."

"Well, that's disappointing. With your survival and all, I thought something would manifest. Perhaps, you haven't given it enough time?"

"I think it would have happened by now, but If anything were to arise, I will inform you immediately, Dr Scholtz."

"As always you are an exemplary professional, Dr Barrett."

That night I did wonder if I had enhanced myself in any way. I pressed the nurse call button to summon Racheal.

"You called? Are you having trouble sleeping?"

"Just a drink of water, please."

Despite the inclination I was disillusioned by the lack of perceived results of my experiment and restrained myself from any form of delusion thereof until three weeks of recuperation had passed and my eventual discharge from the hospital. I stopped in by the supermarket on my way home to purchase some craft beer and a pack of cigarettes. Six beers later my inhibitions had been expelled and my mind began to wonder. I considered that it might well be a lack of realization on my part. I had to attain the appropriate knowledge of my abilities before I could harness them. What I required was illumination, so I made my way to a modern and cosmopolitan bar a few streets along from my flat. I have frequented this bar quite often and regard it as my local on-trade supplier of alcoholic beverages. The people are friendly most of the time and very approachable, which is perfect for the given circumstances. Once I arrived at the bar, I proceeded to order a pint of beer and a dram of whisky and sat at a bar stool next to the bar. I looked to my left and then to my right. Surprisingly, for this classy establishment, I noticed three cocky and belligerent fools talking loudly next to me and began to listen their conversation. I thought of implanting a thought into one of their heads to ascertain if I have a hyperphysical ability, and to what end. I focused in on one of the men and thought, "You my friend are a lowlife piece of scum," this thought appeared to manifest in the man's mind as he withdrew from the conversation temporarily until he reacted by blurting out the statement. Upon doing this, absolute silence followed, two of the three stared at the third, looking angered by his unprovoked insult.

"Why the hell did yam call me a piece of scum, mate?"

"Did I just call you a piece of scum?"

"You did mate and am gonna knock you out for that."

"Rubbish, I didn't call you that mate, you've drunk too much."

"I'm going to knock ya teeth out."

"Calm down mate, calm down. I ain't sure why I said that... but, but I was talking about that lad over there."

The man looked around him to find the intended recipient but quickly lost sight of this idea. From there a fight ensued. The bouncer employed by the bar ran in from outside and restrained one of the men from inflicting a thorough bruising. The next approach I took was to hyperphysically instigate a group of people to get another round of drinks. I looked around the bar and located the perfect candidates. I focused intently on them, with intense concentration I transmitted "Let's get another drink." At that moment, after a slight pause, they all said at the same time, "let's get another drink."

"Okay." One said.

"Sure." Said the other.

Finally, the last member of the group said, "Why not?" Upon coming to accord they walked to the bar and order a round of drinks.

At this very watering hole where the animals congregate to socialise, court and above all else obliterate past indiscretions and rejoice in any semblance of a celebration. I have distinguished myself with a superior faculty causing distinction from my fellow kin, with the capacity as a higher entity to control and enslave these conceited beasts. I must gain perspective, humility and restraint are paramount, I've already overstepped civil law by causing a brawl in this lowly tavern. I did not commit this heinous act of assault, but I was the cause. Therefore, I am as culpable as the offender, yet my act, surpasses the paradigm set forth by our righteous legislators. If law enforcement were to arrest and charge me it would be on the basis of conjecture obliging me to a statutory defence, regardless. It would leave the prosecution with an unenviable task of incriminating me beyond a reasonable doubt – I would be acquitted before the closing arguments. Construal as an accessory to the grievous bodily harm, could be a favourable tact but how could they determine and prove the causal relation between my thought and his action. First of all, they couldn't, secondly, enough of supposition, the evidence would have to be fabricated to implicate me and resoundingly disproven as a result. I would merely be a witness, not innocent one, but a witness none the less. I am above the law. I will not allow the defunct king's court or acts of parliament determine my moral standards, these aristocrats have less of an appreciation of human rights than the underprivileged and more entitlement. Relative laws differ from culture to culture from past to present, these can't be considered as absolute. What I shall utilise as my measure of morality is my own standards, perhaps transcend the very confines of good and evil. Nevertheless, I must impose rules upon myself which encompass hyperphysical occurrences to prevent full blown anarchy.

I do not wish to subjugate people, as I consider this immoral in itself; to completely rob someone of their will would be the ultimate violation of ones being. Without a will we are denigrated to an object of inertia. And, if I were to control their will, they would be nothing more than a conduit, enslaved and deprived of their innermost essence. I couldn't subject someone to that unless necessary, so my general rule will be that every person, and the concurrent situation, I hyperphysically manipulate, will benefit the greatest number of people involved. I am after all a misanthrope with a pulse. The difficulty I have is that my desire will generally not benefit anyone but myself; or certainly a few that share my desire. This wouldn't be considered altruistic in any sense of the word as they would be merely a by-product of my self-gratification. Even if all parties were to profit and I supressed or prevented any immaterial and material gains from the interaction, sacrificing my own motives for a selfless benevolence, I would still inflict injury upon the appropriated, nullifying any benefit, to the extent that it may be irreparable. The nature of my hyperphysical ability renders it as the antithesis of virtuous conduct, leaving me with little choice but to subject the recipients to unpreventable harm to test the limits of my newly acquired capability.

Haven been given permission by Dr Scholtz to conduct an equivocal social experiment on unsuspecting participants in a controlled environment at the laboratory, I proceeded to advertise through the local university publication, and create the right environment. I removed all the furniture from my colleague, Dr Dunbar's office much to his bemusement and dismay, and setup three chairs and a table, one for myself and two for the participants - my chair faced the two participants and the subject's chairs faced each other. Dr Dunbar's office is painted white, so I regard the room as being safe and neutral. Two additions to the room which are completely abnormal is my laboratory assistant, Dr Olivia Munro, sitting in the corner in a straitjacket and a fake handgun on the table – prior to entering the room the participants were told to ignore anything out of the ordinary. Now to the tests. Test one: Subject A and B to release my assistant from the straitjacket, and thereafter restrain my assistant in the straitjacket. Test two: Subject A to fall in love with Subject B, and vice versa. Test three: Subject B to subsequently shoot Subject A. Subject A and B are both twenty-one-year-old males, and most importantly they identify as heterosexual. My colleague is a thirty-two-year-old female, whose sexual preference in a partner is irrelevant.

"Good evening gentleman, my name is Dr Barret, please have a seat. I hope you don't mind but I will refer to you as Subject A and Subject B for the duration of this experiment."

"Subject A what is your first impression of Subject B?"

"I cannot comment on his personality, as we have never met but he has a normal appearance."

"And appears to be unassuming?"

"I think it would be improper of me to make that assertion."

"Very well. Subject B, do you hold yourself in higher esteem than Subject A?"

"Too early to tell."

"I'll take that as a no. How about you Subject A, do you harbour an arrogant attitude?"

"Not that I am aware of."

"Humility is admirable. I wanted to make a point of empathising this from the beginning, a sense of equality between the two of you is the foundation from which we will build."

"Foundation for what?"

"I am being deliberately abstruse for your sake, Subject B."

"I can infer that you are trying to disguise your intent, but I am unable to fathom what that is quite yet."

"You're stating the obvious, but those wits of yours will be exercised. Do you have any prejudices towards any particular community within society Subject A?"

"You are going to have to be more specific."

"The gay community. I want you to be brutally honest."

"I hope this isn't relevant to your research?"

"Why?"

"Because it is a sin, that should be punished by eternal damnation."

"I suppose I shouldn't expect restraint from a fanatic… I presume you are religious Subject A?"

"Yes, I am devout roman catholic. The sheer utterance of homosexuality has made decide to bid you farewell."

"Ah the prevalent monotheism… your god would be displeased. Do have faith Subject A, and refrain from forfeiting payment. Other than proposing the question to Subject B there will be no more mention of homosexuality."

"It's against my better judgement but I shall stay for the time being."

"How about you Subject B?"

"As long as the queers don't come near me, I have no issue with them."

"Superb, discrimination towards this type of orientation is mandatory, otherwise I would have dismissed you without pay, clearly I couldn't put that in writing, but nevertheless you are proving to be the perfect candidates. Let's delve a little deeper, shall we. Subject A, I want you to tell Subject B something about yourself?"

"I am an undergraduate student studying politics."

"Subject B are you politically inclined?"

"No, I have no interest in politics."

"What ambitions do you have in the political sphere Subject A?"

"I hope one day to become a member of parliament and represent my constituency at Westminster."

"Very ambitious, Subject A. Another bigot in the commons is just what this country needs, but don't worry this experiment is confidential, your reputation will remain intact." I winked a couple of times for effect.

"I don't appreciate being called a bigot and I can't ignore that ominous statement and the winking, Dr Barrett. What are you going to do to us?"

"It's more of a question of what you will inflict upon yourself, Subject A. I am merely an observer, studying your behavioural responses to social developments, the impulsivity in which you act in response to psychological changes and the influence of your emotions in relation to your cognition. I purposefully provoked a concern in you about maintaining your dignity, so you are more in tune with your inhibitions encouraging resistance. But fear not, no matter what happens, Subject A, your political eminence shall persevere in the notion of exogenous influence."

"That hasn't reassured me in the slightest."

"I have no issue as long as you don't condition us with electricity."

"Not in the manner in which you conceive, Subject B, but I certainly would like to adopt a method of positive and negative reinforcement, but how feasible that is remains to be seen."

"I for one object to folk psychology but I can't forgo the sum of money offered for my participation so I shall entertain your notions."

"Tremendous Subject B. Moving swiftly on, what hobbies do you pursue, Subject A?"

"I collect obsolete currencies, read and I play cricket."

"How do you collect that?"

"From fellow enthusiasts of course."

"Are these hobbies of any interest to you Subject B?"

"I do enjoy reading and currency is a factor in which I study."

"That's convenient, what are you studying Subject B?"

"Economics."

"Excellent, we have found some common ground between the two of you, however tenuous."

"Is that the purpose of this experiment?"

"That certainly wouldn't be an inaccurate interpretation, Subject B."

I chuckled to myself.

"Okay all pleasantries aside, I am going to leave the room for fifteen minutes, the experiment shall begin when I return. In the meantime, please don't hesitate to get to know each other better."

I am under the impression that my encephalon is an omnidirectional transmitter of gamma rays, with the behaviour of ordinary sinusoidal electromagnetic waves at that end of the spectrum, encoded with frequency modulated data, propagating through air - a non-conducting medium - until it penetrates the subject's skull, invariably damaging whatever may be contained, producing a gamma voltaic conversion triggering electrochemical communication deciphering the message and appropriating the receiver to adopt the instruction - effectively communication through a physical interaction adhering to a physical system. Through inelastic scattering the internal energy of brain matter is then transferred back the photon which is reflected to my brain with recipient's sensory data, emotions, memories, imagery in the mind and the linguistic mental activity of the subject. I strongly believe that this is how the gamma rays will interact with neural tissue. To test this hypothesis, I went through to an adjacent office, which would rule out any suspicions cast upon me, and concentrated intensely. I presupposed that due to the short wavelength and inversely proportional high wave frequency the gamma rays should penetrate through the wall separating us enabling me to broadcast the thoughts, after some time I could distinctly hear them talking which was impossible due to the thickness of the wall.

"What's your opinion of this so far Subject A?"

"After speaking with Dr Barrett, I have become very cynical about the entire thing. On a separate matter, please refrain from calling me Subject A, it is very impersonal, it makes me feel like an object of derision."

"How could it possibly give you that impression?"

"I am very perceptive."

"Overly sensitive you mean. Are we going to address the elephant in the room or what?"

"What do you mean?"

Subject B whispered to Subject A.

"The woman sitting over there in the straitjacket."

"I can hear you and please address me as Dr Munro, and I must say I disapprove of your intolerance you should be ashamed of yourselves."

"Why are you in straitjacket, Dr Munro?"

"Dr Barrett insisted I wear it, apparently its vital to the experiment. I am sure he will explain all when he returns."

Convinced that my theorising is true, I will instigate test one in accordance with the self-imposed directive by implanting thoughts into the subject's head. To aid me in my endeavour I imagined seeing through my colleague's eyes, I thought this possible given that the optical nerve transfers visual data to the brain which should theoretically be accessible. Despite this I was surprised when an image of the room in which she was situated in, vividly appeared in front of my eyes, I could see both Subjects sitting in silence. Body language and facial expressions were crucial to the success of the tests. I transmitted the following to Subject A,

"I believe it to be maltreatment for Dr Munro, who is a woman no less, to be in that straitjacket. I am going to release her."

"Hmmm..."

"What Subject A?"

"I just had a thought. Dr Munro, I find it entirely inappropriate for you to be in a straitjacket do you mind if I untie you?"

"I don't think you should be doing that Subject A."

"I am not talking to you Subject B."

"No, I don't think that's necessary, I'm fine. This is how the experiment is meant to be."

I transmitted another thought.

"I will feel emasculated if I do not help a woman in need. I must release her."

Upon hearing this Subject A stood up and walked over to my colleague. He looked round at Subject B and asked for him to help but Subject B refused to do so. For a short while Subject A stared at my colleague with a perturbed look on his face.

"I am going to help Subject A free Dr Munro." I transmitted to Subject B.

Subject B consequently stood up and walked over to my colleague. Despite her initial protests, they freed my colleague.

"What now Subject A?"

"Did I not make myself clear? Don't call me Subject A, my name is Matt."

"I don't think you should be telling me your name."

"What does it matter."

They all stood in silence unsure of what to do next.

"I might not get paid for releasing the doctor."

I transmitted to Subject A and Subject B.

"Subject A are you thinking what I am thinking?"

"Depends, what are you thinking?"

"I am thinking that we should put the doctor back in the straitjacket."

"I thought the same."

"Would you mind us putting you back in the straitjacket?"

"Not at all, Dr Barrett insisted that I remain in the straitjacket."

My colleague held her arms out, and Subject A and B, fastened my assistant back into the strait jacket. As the two subjects returned to their chairs my colleague sat down in her original place. The objective of Test one achieved. I quickly noted down the result.

There are various treatments of the will that can't account for manipulation. My hyperphysical ability compromises the origin of the will undermining a prominent theory of an era qualifying free will. Let's consider the ancient wisdom of the Greeks. They proposed that the will is a faculty of the mind, that can prompt the body to move and the intellect to consider. The intellect evaluates various options presented and determines what the right course of action is. The will pursues whatever decision that may be. The faculties of intellect and will are unique to a free agent and are the sole properties that distinguish it from inferior instinctual entities. The interaction between the two is a prerequisite to free will. If I made an intellectual intervention and interjected a thought, the criteria for a free agent would still be satisfied, and the interaction sustained. Due to the subject desiring to do what the implanted thought incites them to desire to do, which is interpreted as a subdivision of the prominent action-related desire, based upon an amalgamation of a descendant tree with a corresponding framework for reasoning by virtue of the intellect. Depending on the level of introspection the branching regression could transpire for a considerable length of time. Facilitated by reasoning upon a desire for a desire creating an infrastructure for a set of desires responsive to reason. Not forgoing the capacity to treat the desires as obtrusive and reject them, choosing alternatives as they would if they weren't manipulated hyperphysically; despite the thought itself, seamlessly transitioned into the process, disguised all the while as that of their own.

Excluding, for the time being, the more oppressive coercion, influence is detrimental to the crux of theory. Amongst other external influences an impressionable mind may adopt a desire to emulate their idol, presenting a favourable outcome to the intellect, assessed through prejudiced reasoning. Opting for this desire could potentially forgo their true desire, withholding free will, conventionally speaking, an independent choice. An intensive indoctrinated ideology may be thrust upon a naive and susceptible individual. With a weak constitution they may be persuaded that a prescribed set of desires are what they ought to have, and a volition that should only be exercised on command. The individual may well be astute at reasoning but if effectively manipulated the judgement inferred will be prepossessed to a contrived eventuality. An objective convert who has subjected the principles and values to well-reasoned analysis and who now chooses to recruit others, convinced that the will of a missionary is a will they want, and if this desire were to become their will, the conditions are fulfilled for a lineage complex. Yet, the preacher is no more acting through free will than the preached causing only the ignominy that they once suffered. Coerced through false prophecies, posthumous salvation, and poignant parables to induce the fear of God; they desire once more to be just and righteous like their messiah or deities entirely devoid of their own will and cause.

Tenuous as this may be my hyperphysical ability exposes further deficiencies in the theory. In particular, if I were to compel Subject B to kill Subject A, it may not be enough to implant an action-related desire without any foundation. I would have to address the network of reason responsive desires, systematically associating himself with the transpiring act of will, such as identifying as a murderer and spending a lifetime in prison, to name a few branches. However, murder is not always premeditated, if I can instigate an irrational reaction to Subject A's behaviour and rhetoric towards him, I may enforce a momentary contradiction in his reasoning and character. He would still engage his intellect, but it would be guided by my deviant logic, appropriating his resultant will. This form of methodical brainwashing mischievously preserves the interaction between the faculties required by the Greek philosophers for free will, yet in no uncertain terms could we attribute free will to the agent. Hijacked, the free agent's self-determining capacity for evaluating an appropriate choice would be dependent on my inclination, denigrating him to a conduit devoid of free will. In the event that the subject is super resistant, ignoring most of the fleeting desires that cross his mind, selectively choosing based upon acquired tastes and etiquette. I would have to get creative and delve a little deeper into his subjectivity locating various beliefs, prejudices, memories and acquired knowledge, manipulating these impressions to my advantage.

A plausible solution would be to insert a clause whereby the source of the generated desire is innate or a genetic predisposition independent from nurture and inseparable from our nature. What is right is what is true to our self, irrespective of the moral implications of that choice. This would impart greater emphasis upon the unconscious instincts abolishing our beloved reasoning, which is no longer considered trustworthy, for a more intuitive approach. It is hard to consider the intellect to be surpassed by such a senseless endeavour, but to ensure the sanctimony of the self and the free will thereof, this may be the only solution available to the lesser entities in the face of a superior being equipped with a hyperphysical ability. In the event that this superhuman was a tyrant, they could rise up to usurp the established order – the tyranny of the many – and deliver the people to a totalitarian dystopia; and if this reality were to befall them they would have no realisation that this silent revolution had occurred.

Test two is going to be far more challenging as the feeling of love is inherently a chemical reaction to sensory stimuli, but I shall not be defeated that easily, as those who have never experienced love have the capacity to have mental representations, and if lucid enough, it may stimulate a chemical response in the beholder. Before resorting to the invention of these superficial substitutes, I will appeal to memories, mental states, and feelings that he has associated with love throughout his life and then project them onto Subject B, this act of deception may lead to an alteration of the sexual orientations of Subject A and his prejudices towards the corresponding sexual behaviour. A more intimate love manifested through sexual attraction and physical contact is a requisite as they must have a strong aversion and naturally resist demonstrating the effectiveness of my power. I projected a thought to Subject A.

"I miss my girlfriend I wish she was here."

I had no idea if he had a girlfriend or not but took the chance on an assumption.

"Oh Beckie, how I adore you." Thought Subject A.

Projected against the wall, I began to see experiences that he had with Beckie, some of which were vulgar pornographic dalliances together, exposing this devout acolyte. In the name of research, I had to witness it all, however distasteful. Cunningly I began to periodically insert various thoughts to develop a connection to Subject B.

"Subject B has very attractive facial features. Beckie doesn't compare to this handsome man. I should approach him to find out if he is single. I would like to go on a few dates with him to see if we are compatible before having sexual relations with him."

With that I had exhausted my resources. A matter of minutes passed as Subject A was suspended in disbelief at the accompanying thoughts to the imagery that was streaming through his mind or so I believed. I anticipated some sort of reaction, but nothing happened. I made a second attempt but was briefly interrupted.

"You okay Subject A? You look deep in thought almost as if you're in a trance."

"He is very observant and caring; those are qualities I look for in a man. He would make the perfect partner perhaps even a lover. I wonder if he is well endowed." I transmitted to Subject A.

As a heterosexual man I was beginning to cringe at my own mischief, but Subject A took this a step further by slamming his head off the table near knocking himself out. He fell off his chair onto the floor and laid in the foetal position whining. I may have pushed him too far. My assistant struggled to her feet and came to his aid the best she could. Subject B was trying to repress his laugher.

"That's going to leave a bruise."

"Have you no empathy, Subject B. Get me out of this straitjacket."

Subject B released my assistant.

"Let me have a look at you, Subject A."

"Come on Subject A, I will help you to your feet and guide you to your seat." Subject A complied.

"I think I am beginning to fall in love with this thoughtful and considerate man. We would live happily together for the rest of our lives." I implanted in Subject A's mind.

The shock of what I imagined to be an intrusion in his most private and intimate space by none other than his own inner monologue caused his face to go pale and for him to put his head in his hands. Humiliated by his own mind he was on the verge of sobbing. I thought I would give Subject A, a brief reprieve and concentrate on Subject B, perhaps he would be more susceptible. I transmitted a thought.

"Subject A is cute. I find his vulnerability alluring; it is almost if he needs someone to love and care for him and I wish to be that person."

Subject B was laughing manically, Subject A was in the depths of despair and my colleague looked very uncomfortable, borderline scared, in that room with the two lunatics. Subject B finally snapped out of it and approached Subject A.

"Someone needs a hug."

"Get off me, that is not appropriate you imbecile."

Despite his stature Subject A was able to fend off Subject B and the room fell silent. Subject A seeing an opportunity made a dash for the door, he pulled and turned at the handle only to discover that it was locked by yours truly, however much it troubled me to victimise all three participants, it is imperative to conclude the objectives of the experiment to ascertain what I am truly capable of.

"Why is the door locked Dr Munro?"

"I don't know, I assume Dr Barrett didn't want you to leave until he returns."

"If you don't let me out, I will kick the door down."

"And forfeit payment?"

"Thanks for reminding me, I will stay for the time being."

"Wow, your easily persuaded by monetary gain."

Enough of this I thought.

"I will examine Subject A's face to find if I am attracted to him."

"Why are you looking at me like that, Subject B?"

"I was just examining your face to see if I was attracted to you. I mean... well that was a Freudian slip."

"And do you?"

"I find Subject A very attractive." I transmitted.

"Yes Dr Munro, I fancy Subject A."

"That's wonderful Subject B. Don't you want find out if the feeling is mutual?"

"Oh dear, I guess so, Dr Munro."

The rate in which Subject B accepted the thoughts was remarkable but Subject A treated the thoughts as foreign and invasive, rejecting them and refusing to associate himself with what I implanted, which I had expected from both candidates given their profile. I implanted another thought.

"I think I should propose to Subject A that we kiss to see if there is any chemistry between us."

"For once I am going to follow my head instead of my heart, Dr Munro. Subject A, I mean Matt, I think we should kiss."

"Have you lost your mind?"

Subject B having the bigger stature descended upon Subject A with his lips pursed and planted a thorough kiss which he painfully prolonged which I presumed was through some misplaced passion.

"That proves it I am in love with Matt" I transmitted to Subject B.

"Wow, Matt, I can't believe it, but I think I am in love with you."

As is to be expected, without electrodes attached to his scalp, the physiological aspect, the release of chemicals in the central dopamine pathways, is indeterminate but the behaviour of Subject B suggests that there may have been a release, or that a release was not necessary in the conversion of implemented thought or desire to will. However, it could have been a shallow infliction, a mere command to which he obeyed without any deep introspection; a thought without any profound affects upon the psyche and the emotions, which I regard to be necessary for a successful implantation. Furthermore, his susceptibility to a generated thought may transcend the actual influence of the implantation itself, which is also evident in Subjects A rejection of the generated thoughts. The result of test two is inconclusive mainly due to Subject A's resistance. Had I initiated a feeling of love or even an impulse towards Subject B the test could be considered to be successful. But having some more susceptible than others calls into question the effectiveness of the hyperphysical ability. I knew the perfect method to initiate test three.

"Matt knows that I kissed him and that I am now a homosexual, I will have to kill him before he tells anyone. There is a gun on the table. I should pick it up and shoot him point blank."

This triggered an immediate reaction and Subject D walked over to the gun to shoot the man he had just declared his love for. Returning to rational state of mind upon pulling the trigger he realised the gun was fake, so he threw it down approached the door and began to kick it in. I rushed from my office and opened the door before he got the chance to kick it in.

"What is happening? Why are you kicking the door?"

Subject B's face expressed a look of shame.

"I must get out of here Dr Barrett."

"Okay Subject B, I am going to postpone the experiment to another day given that you were kicking the door down. I will provide you with a date and time. You both can go home now."

"Are we getting paid?"

"Yes, Subject A, please see the secretary on the way out. She has an envelope for you which contains your payment."

Both Subjects left the room. I was slightly concerned with what might happen once they are on their own. So, I quickly phoned the secretary and had her schedule separate follow up sessions. At these sessions neither participant could explain what had happened and didn't want to talk about it any further. I cancelled the experiment. Of course, this was a means to cover up the real experiment which was a borderline success with the exception of Subjects A's reluctance to accept the thoughts I implanted. I asked my assistant if she would like to join me for an alcoholic beverage later that night so I could get to know her better but to also establish that what I perceived to be happening in the room was actually taking place, this was crucial. She agreed to do so, without any gentle persuasion. An additional objective that I will attend to whilst at the bar is to surpass thoughts and go directly for action. I ordered her preferred poison, to my delight was an Old Fashioned with a robust smoky scotch at the core. I took mine neat with a pint of beer. We got to talking. She gave a detailed portrayal of the events that took place which coincided with what I perceived to be happening. To my relief it was acknowledgement that I wasn't delusional.

"I still can't believe I had to cancel the experiment because one of the candidates inexplicably fell in love with the other."

"And without reciprocation."

"Poor guy."

"I would have more sympathy had he not violated Subject A."

My assistant began to digress into her hobbies, her new flat and I am not sure what else as I began to lose focus on her chatter and instead sipped on my refreshing pint of beer. She eventually excused herself to go to the toilet, presenting me with opportunity to control another human being's actions. I scanned the bar discerning an appropriate target and fixated on a man and a woman sitting at a booth. I focused intensely trying to prompt her to move to the middle of the bar to a relatively empty space, it took some time, but she arose from her seat, wandered over to the spot I had chosen and stood suspended until she regained her faculties as I relinquished. The man got up and walked over to her.

"Darling, where are you going? I hadn't finished my story."

"I do apologise dear; I am not sure why I walked over here."

They both resumed the conversation as if nothing had happened. Not content by this, I concentrated on the man and had him move to the exact same spot. He did as I intended. The woman inquisitively followed behind him.

"What are you doing dear?"

Again, I relinquished.

"I'm not sure, I think I was trying to figure out what you were looking at."

To my astonishment they returned to their seats and continued chatting oblivious to the compelling force sitting at the bar across from them. I have now surpassed the reason responsive desire framework, for they had good reason not to walk to that spot, one being that it was pointless, and in the process not only denying the subject free will but free action.

Dr Munro returned from the toilet, and we chatted for a bit before she excused herself once more but this time to depart for home. We exchanged goodbyes, she went in for a hug, which I obliged. I offered to walk her home, but she said it wasn't necessary, so I stayed at the bar and proceeded to get heavily drunk on beer and whisky. The bar closed and I was the last one to leave. I stumbled along the street in the direction of my flat. Without looking I crossed the road; in that instance I heard a car honk its horn and abruptly apply the brakes to which I heard a screech, I looked towards the oncoming vehicle and instinctively imagined myself stopping it. The front of the car crushed on impact and the driver was ejected through the windscreen, I was unscathed. The theory I conceived of in my drunken state is that the momentum of the gamma radiation from my brain can overcome the electromagnetic forces binding the atoms of an object. Rather than separating the object into its constituent parts, the entire object moves along with the atoms it is composed of. The hyperphysical force, which gives me the power of telekinesis, has the capacity to manipulate the physical system in which we find ourselves. I checked that there were no witnesses present and made a hasty exit from the scene.

I woke up the following morning to the immediate flashback of the night before, I witnessed all over again the horrors of what could be the first fatality. My initial reaction was to tune into the news channel on the television for a report of the incident. Whilst I watched, I necked two paracetamols, drank a gallon of water, and smoked a cigarette to overcome my intolerable hangover. The night before will be my last dalliance with alcohol given that I stumbled upon a life-or-death situation and reacted with all the dexterity of a drunk. I turned my attention back to the television screen.

"Here is Wilfred Hancock with the latest report from the scene."

"Thank you, Jenny. A fatal car accident occurred last night on the intersection of Clarence Drive and Hyndland road in west end of the city. Where one man, who can't be identified at this time, has tragically lost his life. The media attention surrounding the incident, has led to a press conference being held by detective chief superintendent Archie Hamilton."

"Good morning, members of the press. The circumstances surrounding the incident are bizarre to say the least, there appears to have been a collision involving one car but what it struck is a mystery. There is no debris to indicate that another car was involved and there are no obstructions in the middle of the road that it could have hit. There are no surveillance cameras operating in this area but there is a relatively high frequency of people using this road at the given time, so I appeal to the public for any witnesses to come forward with information. This will be crucial to our investigation. Thank you."

I turned off the television. I was stunned; I couldn't believe I had killed someone and was now subject to a homicide investigation. Paranoid stricken, I hatched a plan to go into seclusion hoping that the investigation doesn't turn up any identifying clues or testimony from a witness implicating me as the murderer. I of course have a means to supress this – apprehending the witness before the trial and coercing them into recanting their story. As for the implausible physical evidence, I would brainwash my way into the police station and remove it. Once I'm safely ensconced in a remote location, I will obsessively follow the developments of the case on the news.

Chapter 4
The Visitors

I made my way through the laboratory until I reached Dr Scholtz office and knocked on the door.

"Who is it?"

"Dr Barrett."

"Do come in."

"How are you today?"

"Very well. This may come as a shock to you, but I am handing in my resignation notice."

"For what reason?"

"I failed my life's ambition; it would be an exercise in futility to continue."

"Dr Barrett, you expect me to just let you leave with the knowledge you possess?"

"I had a feeling you would complicate matters, but you will not stand in the way of my retirement."

Dr Scholtz opened the drawer of his desk and pulled out a syringe. I allowed a chase around the office to ensue for comic relief, and to deceive, but when I tired of this, I implanted a thought into Dr Scholtz mind.

"I will not chase Dr Barrett and inject him."

Dr Scholtz halted immediately and stared at me.

"I will permit Dr Barrett to resign as he is a close friend but on the condition that he will not break the confidentiality agreement."

"Something odd is happening here."

"What do you mean Dr Scholtz?"

"I should be killing you."

I implanted another thought in a similar vein as the last one.

"Dr Barrett, I may have changed my mind... but I can't be certain."

"Well, have a good think about it."

"My mind is set; I will spare Dr Barrett's life and banish him from this organization, with the penalty of death should he return."

"Get out of my sight, Dr Barrett, if you return, I will kill you."

The fierce sun relinquished its hold on the day, diminishing into soft rays, eclipsing the blue of the sky with a flamboyant radiant display. I admired the sunset for a further 10 minutes before departing to my parent's house. Once behind the wheel, I contemplated how to make an income by committing fraud, through setting up a business, brainwashing unsuspecting people into purchasing unnecessary products, and becoming a millionaire. I am of course aware of the nature of consumerism, and perhaps I should not classify this as fraud but as entrepreneurship. The particulars of the scheme are to organise a team of tech nerds, and take full ownership, to design and develop a tablet computer and software applications to contend with the tech giants and corner the market. My competitors too have the invention of the tablet computer among their catalogue of gadgets rendering it worthless, and if the development by my team lacks innovation and originality, I will resort to brainwashing customers into purchasing the device until the popularity is to the extent whereby a rival or investors, also through manipulation, during the floatation of my company on the stock market, will make an acquisition of my prestigious companies shares paying out a large sum that I can retire on. It goes against the very principled restrictions I set out. If this were to fail, I would return to lecturing at the university.

"Hello, Ian and Gwendoline."

"Oh, thank god, my dear son is home."

"You will find no hope in your superstitions mother."

"What are you talking about? Come have a cup of tea."

"Hello father. I have some news, I resigned from my job at the pharmaceutical company."

"I suppose you will profit from the taxation of my hard work with your unemployment benefits."

"Don't be ridiculous Ian, I have a vast amount of savings, to pay my mortgage and utility bills. What has devastated me was returning that divine car, but I have sought a replacement, a Land Rover, a fine example of the ingenuity of engineering by the automobile manufacturers."

"Good lad. You finally realised your overcompensating for your inadequacies."

"What you lack in charm you make up for in rudeness, you bitter old man."

I conversed with my parents about trivial matters before informing them of my log cabin retreat for two weeks to the loch north of the city. I provided them with the address in case they wanted to visit, and should they call, I assured them I would have cell reception. I departed their abode and drove along the motorway, with a shifting stream of consciousness, I arrived at the cabin. I settled in very quickly and monitored the news channels. At intervals I diverted my attention with a masterful work of fiction and long leisurely walks through the forest. I even went for a swim in the loch, breast stroking my way out into deep waters. However, I could not acclimatise to the temperature of the water even after a rigorous exercise, so I hastily front crawled my way back to shoreline never to repeat.

"Breaking news, a witness has come forward in the case that has now been dubbed, 'The Act of God', during the interview I had with Mrs Partridge, she claimed the police dismissed her portrayal of events, describing it as fantastical story that without doubt was an impossibility. They even suggested she seek help from the mental health services. Here is the exclusive interview with Mrs Partridge… what happened on the night of June the twenty first?"

"I was watering my orchids on my window cell when I looked out the window and saw a man stumbling along the street, he crossed the road with an oncoming car which crashed into some sort of force field surrounding him. I think it was divine intervention. I have never seen anything like it."

"Could you identify the man if you were to see him again?"

"Yes."

I turned off the television. The predicament of a positive identification now plagued the back of my mind even with the discrediting of the witness's statement by law enforcement. I retired to my bed to reinvigorate my troubled mind. I woke up to a man standing over me, with a knife in his hand, which he put to my neck.

"Bind his hands and legs."

They carried me to the living room and sat me down on a chair.

"You're quite the master of deception, Dr Barrett."

"How did you know I was here, Dr Scholtz?"

"I paid a visit to your parents; they were quite willing to talk when I applied a little pressure."

"I will kill you for that."

"I heard about your little escapade on the news, I immediately knew it was you, Dr Barrett. You are going to divulge any information that isn't on this external hard drive you provided us with, and if you don't then I see no other option but to torture and kill you."

"You brought the hard drive? What a fool."

I possessed one of the henchmen and had him walk over to Dr Scholtz and stab him in the stomach. He dropped to the floor covered in blood.

"Robert, what have you done?"

"I don't know what happened, Jimmy. I…"

I had Robert set upon the other cohort. He slashed at him wildly cutting his raised arm. Jimmy adopted some sort of martial arts kick which sent Robert through the air landing through the glass table. I appropriated Jimmy, had him approach Robert, pick up his knife and stab him in the chest repeatedly. The last gruesome act I would commit, is to have Jimmy pull the knife out of Robert's chest and with one swift movement slice his own throat. I stood up from the chair and hopped over to the blade. Lay on the ground next to the knife so I could get a hold of it and sliced through the zip ties. I had to dispose of the three bodies, but I had no shovel. As dawn arose, I left the gruesome scene and drove to the garden centre and petrol station at the local town; purchased a shovel, some matches and gasoline. Unlike the mentor Dr Scholtz, I did not consider the lime to be necessary, but I did emulate his method. The subsequent hours were spent cleaning up blood, removing any signs of violence and wrapping the bodies in linen and moving them to the boot of my car. Under the shade of darkness, deep in the forest I went. I toiled at digging a large grave for several hours, dropped in the bodies one by one, plus the knife, and covered up the burial site. I pre-emptively took the keys from Jimmy's pocket, drove their car to a remote location, doused it with gasoline, and set it on fire. All I could do was hope that I covered any trace of this atrocity.

I spent three unremorseful days lazing about in doors, but they weren't without hardship, my cravings for that mystery pill had become more acute over time causing the occasional grinding of the teeth whilst I climbed the walls, "This will pass" I would tell myself, I thought it best to go for a walk. I lost my bearings and ventured far away from my cabin. It began to get dark. In poor judgement I climbed a tree to get a better vantage point. I saw the lights from the local town on the horizon, if I could make it there, I could find my way back. Holding on for dear life I looked up at the sky and became mesmerised by a frantically moving light, it could not be a star I thought nor any ordinary flying object. It began to get closer and closer until I was confronted by an amazing array of lights. To my astonishment it was an alien spaceship, or at the very least an avant-garde military aircraft. It hovered awhile then swung from side to side as if the pilot was having a seizure, took a curved trajectory down to earth, rapidly changed direction, hovered again and then descended to the forest floor. Naturally, I was curious, with great difficulty I climbed down from the tree and walked in the direction of the landing of what I had resolved to be extra-terrestrials. After a few hours of searching, a distrust of the senses prompted an incisive scepticism about the entire experience, it must have been a drug induced flashback from the medication, but I could not recall anything about aliens. Disillusioned, with no point of reference, I chose a direction and made haste back to the cabin. I came across a large patch of vegetation, struggled to get through it, but with a push, I tumbled and landed on my knees. I gradually lifted my head and to my surprise there was a large arrangement of lights shining in my general direction, as my eyes adjusted, I bared witness to an alien spacecraft.

Fearful of their advanced weaponry, I took refuge behind a bush and peered over. This encounter held great significance and had to be approached tactfully with caution, for my actions will influence their perception of my race, but I was desperate to meet the aliens, the knowledge they bestow must be beyond comprehension. After much deliberation I felt suitably prepared with my hyperphysical ability for hostility, in the form of inquisitive probing or outright violence, but I maintained a hope that the extra-terrestrials are affable creatures. I searched for an entrance but to no avail. I adopted a more effective strategy. I focused on the interior of the spacecraft and imagined looking through the eyes of the alien. What I saw astounded me. The alien's comrade looked like a hairy brown arachnid, very strange indeed. A chest cavity opened, two arms came out and it proceeded to press buttons on the control interface. What was more unsettling was the six prickly legs. I was intrigued by their appearance but envisaged that it would be prejudicial to the integration of our two civilisations if we chose to co-exist. I approached the spacecraft and gave it a couple of bangs with my fist, at first nothing transpired so I kept knocking until a ramp descended from the spacecraft. In a matter of seconds, the alien had confronted me, but I was able to suspend its movement.

Examining the alien, I inadvertently touched the leg which I immediately regretted as the prickly hairs stung my hand causing it to throb with pain. Hyperphysically, I had the alien open its mosaic sack for a chest so I could examine his two hands. Attached to the hand was four fingers and an opposable thumb, exactly like a human. The alien appeared to be an amalgamation of earthly creatures. I continued the inspection but refrained from ascertaining its gender as it may not react to kindly to me embarrassing it. I looked around the rest of the alien which was well protected by its six legs and hardened body. There really wasn't much else to see. It had two eyes but no discernible face, two nose holes and a mouth. Since the Arachnids can breathe without any aid or breathing apparatus, it leads me to believe that the atmosphere of their planet must have similar composition to earth.

Investigation of the spaceship was the next protocol. At the very least the discovery of weapons of mass destruction will indicate their intentions. I walked up the cliché ramp and into the spacecraft. What a machine of innovation and wonder, beyond my novice understanding, even an earthly engineer couldn't fathom the technology. Distracted I accidentally released one of the aliens. It approached me in a flash from outside the spacecraft, but I caught it just in time before it could inflict damage upon me, or perhaps it just wanted to examine me, either way I didn't want to find out. Whilst I had the aliens under control, they started communicating with each other, I presumed they were discussing the matters at hand, the correlation between the paralysis and this strange creature that was knocking on their door. I was too fascinated by the spacecraft to make enquiries. Attached to a rack on the wall was a collection of guns, suspicious as this may be, I still maintained hope that diplomacy and peace could prevail.

One last objective before communication is quarantine. I could not risk them contracting a virus, even the flu could prove to be fatal, given the unproven effectiveness of their immune response to earthily diseases. I had both aliens under my control, yet I did not know how to switch off the spacecraft lights, I looked at the aliens and then the buttons, as I was about to push one the aliens exclaimed "wooha" until they let out an almighty "bing bong," which gave me the impression they knew what I was trying to do. I clicked the button and the lights turned off. I vacated the area with the aliens in tow, with the intention of leaving the spacecraft in seclusion amongst the trees. Under the cover of darkness, I had both aliens follow me through the forest back to my cabin, getting there proved a challenge, but we remained undetected for the duration of the hike. Too large to fit through the front door, I opted for settlement in the garage. I took the television from the living room, plugged it in, and connected my laptop through a HDMI cable so I could undertake teaching the aliens English, but first one week of separation. I resolved to remain awake for the seven days as my grip may falter if I am unconscious. Observations gave me the impression that the arachnids were determined not to sleep too, the tension was palpable. I routinely fed the aliens by slipping vegetables through the adjoining door between the kitchen and the garage.

A popular time of the year to be at one with nature, my charm had not diminished, the owner of the cabin, extended my stay by six weeks.

"Hello, my name is Ethan." I pointed to myself.

The arachnids looked puzzled. I pointed again. They looked at each other.

"Hello, my name is Click, Click, Buzz."

The other alien wasn't such a quick learner, but he got their eventually.

"Hello, my name is Click, Click, Buzz, Zing."

I proceeded to teach them English through a translation application on my computer, it incorporated images and sounds to aid in apprehension and pronunciation. The progress they made was phenomenal, but I noticed that one student had a far superior intellect compared to his comrade. I figured that Click, Click Buzz, Zing must be the brawn to Click, Click, Buzz's brains. The perfect scouting party.

"We are fatigued, Ethan, we must sleep."

"You are impressing me, Click, Click, Buzz. I shall not harm you, please sleep. I shall return in the morning."

"How long does darkness last on your planet?"

"It varies with the seasons, but I will say nine hours."

"An hour is made up of sixty minutes of which is made up of sixty seconds and there is nine hours. Okay, I think I understand."

"If in doubt refer to the segment on time that we covered earlier."

The arachnids fell asleep which presented me with the perfect opportunity to get some rest. I locked the garage preventing escape, and if they should try, I would be alerted by the destruction of the door.

"Do you eat animals on your planet?"

"Yes."

"Great, Click, Click, Buzz, I have prepared you a hearty breakfast, a nice rump steak."

They devoured the steak and went straight back to their English lessons. One month later and they were practically fluent. I tested the radius of my hyperphysical control over the arachnids on my journeys to the supermarket to buy groceries, I wore a face mask and gloves as a precaution. The distance of the emissions I could get was incredible and they clearly diffracted around obstacles to the desired target which was a phenomenon in and of itself.

"I have a pertinent question Click, Click, Buzz. Why have you come to earth?"

"I would like to talk about the ongoing pollution of your environment that we witnessed on your laptop."

"Perhaps I shouldn't have shown you that… Industry is at the heart of our economy, disavowed by the masses due to its utility, resulting in harmful gases being released into the atmosphere absorbing heat and radiation from the sun warming the earth's atmosphere, causing the ice caps to melt, rising water throughout our coastlines, and droughts in other areas, and adversely affecting the intensity and patterns of our weather."

"Are you not concerned you bring about your own extinction?"

"Deeply, but what can one man do."

"I would also like to know about the nature of humans. You are familiar with your own nature?"

"What can I say, we are intelligent apes; with all the characteristics of an animal, inhibited by our intellectual aptitude and flawless logic. Constructive and peaceful most of the time, we are tempted to war through political ideals, territorial expansion in the form of colonialism and seizure of resources."

"War... No war on my native land."

"There has never been civil war in your country?"

"No civil war on my planet."

"That's hard to believe. Are your land masses separated by ocean?"

"There is only one continent."

"You must have an interesting culture?" "We have one art form that we dedicate our life's to mastering, combat, and a principle scientific discipline, the combination and application of physics and mathematics in aerospace engineering."

"What about agriculture, Click, Click, Buzz?"

"We have farmers that tend to and harvest crops and hunting and gathering expeditions."

"Do you fish the oceans?"

"We have rather primitive wooden boats compared to your ships, but they serve the purpose combined with our nets."

"I couldn't help but notice how advanced your spacecraft is."

"That is our principal focus, to seek new worlds to prolong our civilisation, and accommodate our ever-growing population."

"A yes, the ultimate aspiration for an organic being, immortality. I have a theory… but for another day. In the meantime, a similar solution to herd immunity is the only probable means by which I will accomplish my objective, akin to your own enterprise. Do you commit all your intellectual pursuit to paper?"

"Only in our minds, Ethan."

"That's a shame, lost to the ages. I have a request; can you take me back to your planet?"

"This seems like an appropriate time… You have a great power, Ethan. Do all humans possess this power to control others?"

"Only I."

"You can come with us to our planet under one condition, you abstain from using your power."

"Agreed, all I seek is temporary asylum from the law. I shall have to return to earth in the future when I feel adequately prepared to overcome the adversities I now face. I have a quick question I would like to raise which may lead to more. What is the flight duration from earth to your home planet?"

"Based upon your calendar, three years."

"How do you travel so fast?"

"Click, Click, Buzz, Zing and I were stationed at a top-secret facility with an observatory located atop a mountainous terrain, designated with the task of figuring out how to defeat an enemy with as little casualties as possible and exploring our galaxy. Thus, I invented the cloaking device for our spaceship that allowed us to enter your atmosphere undetected, but it malfunctioned hence why we landed. For millennia, our civilisation has prepared to invade another world outside of our galaxy, but we didn't have the technology to get there. The astronomy aspect of our research led me to a fortuitous discovery of a wormhole under the perfect gravitational conditions created by a supermassive blackhole in its proximity. We did this by mapping out the orbit of the surrounding stars until we noticed a deviation, whereby the gravitational pull of a star on the opposite side of the wormhole caused a fluctuation. We prepped our spaceship and embarked on the perilous journey which brought us here, to your galaxy and world."

"Truly remarkable. Excluding your cleverness, I admire your honesty. An unrelated question but what sort of supplies do you have aboard your ship?"

"Thermostabilised and rehydratable organic food, and water."

"Enough for three passengers?"

"Yes, we should have enough."

"Do you have medicine in case I get sick?"

"Yes, we have medical bays in our military bunkers with skilled diagnostics and treatment."

"Do you have other species on your planet?"

"Yes, we have other species."

"Are they harmful?"

"They are not harmful to us as we are superior."

"Are the other species intelligent?"

"They don't have the intellect of my kind; they are very much instinctual."

"Do you have a functioning government?"

"Yes."

"I would like to meet your leader."

"We have more than one leader, the supreme chieftains are deities that we worship and through communion ascertain our purpose. We have shamans within our society that communicate with them through ritual."

"I thought you were a scientific community?"

"We have a profound understanding of the divine."

"That's a glaring inconsistency. On a sperate note, I presume your world is overpopulated?"

"A mother can give birth to up to ten offspring at any given time, so we control and limit the number of births. We haven't outgrown our world, but it is inevitable."

"How do you power your military and medical bunkers?"

"Nuclear energy."

"Nuclear capabilities… I take it you also have an arsenal of nuclear bombs?"

"Ethan, I have been forth coming with my answers but this I cannot say."

"It's okay, I have the capability of inferring."

"Ethan, Click, Click, Buzz, Zing wants to discuss something with me, excuse us."

Click, Click, Buzz was reprimanded, clearly inferior in rank.

"Click, Click, Buzz, Zing is essentially a general of the army, he has no expertise in scientific matters only combat, which I think affects his judgement, especially when it comes to an alliance. We can trust you, Ethan?"
"My intentions are good, I shall inflict no harm upon your kind."

I desired female companionship for my expedition. The most suitable candidate I could think of is my assistant Dr Munro. She is attractively built and has a keen intellect. There is a high probability that she will have a hysterical reaction to the visitors especially given their unnerving appearance. I would have to calm and reassure her that they are friendly, posing no threat. Despite this, I have confidence she would come to terms with, adapt and comprehend the significance of the encounter expeditiously, but what poses an even greater dilemma is persuading her through reason alone to join me in jettisoning off to a distant world with a pair of outlandish and intimidating extra-terrestrials. I felt it necessary for her to have the capacity to make her own choice without my influence after all I was asking her to sacrifice many years of her life. I searched for her name through my contacts on my mobile and gave her a call.

"Hello Dr Munro, its Dr Barrett."

"This is a surprise."

"A pleasant one I hope?"

"Yes, of course. I thought I would let you know that I have been reassigned to a new project."

"That's wonderful news. Dr Munro I have a favour to ask."

"I must know what it is before I can commit."

"I am currently on a cabin retreat at the loch. I was wondering if you could meet me here, I can provide you with the address?"

"For what reason, Dr Barrett?"

"So, we can socialise over a few beverages and perhaps a barbecue, I checked the weather forecast and it should be sunny this weekend."

"That sounds nice."

"Say, this Saturday at noon?"

"I will see you then Dr Barrett."

I walked to the garage to check on the aliens.

"Dr Barrett, Click, Click, Buzz, Zing and I are wondering, why the delay to our departure?"

"I want a female companion to accompany me."

"You want to reproduce on our planet? That's a little inappropriate."

"That is not the only purpose for a female, Click, Click, Buzz."

"Dr Barrett we were in the process of commencing a peace treaty and now you want to bring a warrior?"

"Nor combat, I just want a friend who I can share the experience with."

"I could understand if she was a soldier, some of our most skilful fighters are female but this is pathetic Dr Barrett."

"Did you not require the companionship of Click, Click, Buzz, Zing to come to earth?"

"He is my superior in rank I had no choice but to bring him."

"You're quite the maverick."

"We will permit the woman to come on the grounds that you consider developing a friendship of greater importance than our two civilisations coming to accord."

"Now, now Click, Click, Buzz, you are miss representing the situation, I feel a woman's perspective will be advantageous in our negotiations."

"Certainly, we will await her presence."

Later that day.

"I know what this barbecue needs to get it ignited, some gasoline."

"Hello Dr Barrett, who are you talking to?"

"Just thinking out loud and call me Ethan, do you mind if I address you by your first name, it is a little more cordial?"

"Sure."

"Step back Olivia, I have doused the charcoal with fuel."

"Isn't that dangerous?"

"Not in the right hands. Jesus Christ, I think I have singed my eyebrows."

"You never fail to amaze me, Ethan."

"I am fool, I should have known better... A succulent Burger with all the necessary accompaniments?"

"Sounds delicious."

"A little burnt but edible. Olivia, I have an ulterior motive for asking you here."

"You're not going to hit on me, are you?"

"Do you believe in extra-terrestrials?"

"Is that your attempt at flirtation?"

"No Olivia, answer the question."

"Yes, it's probable."

"And would you like to meet them?"

"I suppose."

"Great, I have two extraordinary..."

I could not reveal the existence of the extra-terrestrials in the garage. I had to protect her from the profound encounter to maintain her ordinary life without disturbing the very fabricate of her reality.

I would have to undertake the journey alone.

"Gentle... creatures it's time to depart."

"No woman?"

"She would have been a liability."

We set off post haste for the spacecraft.

"Click, Click, Buzz, I have no idea where to go."

"Are you prone to forgetting where you park?"

"Mocking me won't endear me to you."

"Click, Click, Buzz, Zing and I through our extensive training are proficient trackers and navigators. If you permit us the ability to move we will guide you there."

"Okay, but no funny stuff."

"Now that we have absconded to your spacecraft. How do you propose to fix the cloaking device Click, Click, Buzz?"

"I have all the necessary parts it shouldn't take too long."

A few hours later.

"I'm curious, do you mind if I observe the take-off procedure?"

"I see no harm in doing so."

I witnessed the complex flight setup trying my utmost to remember it.

Chapter 5
The Final Frontier

"Wait, Click, Click, Buzz, where is my extravehicular mobility unit with life support?"

"Please elaborate, Dr Barrett?"

"My spacesuit?"

"Not necessary, Dr Barrett. A mixture of oxygen and nitrogen derived from its liquid form in a system of tanks pumped into the cabin maintain a pressure of fourteen pounds per square inch which in relation to earth should be consider normal atmospheric pressure."

"What about the g-force I will experience? Do I need to be strapped in? And what if I blackout?"

"Maximum three Gs, insufficient to knock you out, and negligible enough to exert a force on you. Just relax and have pleasant journey."

"I'm curious, is this spacecraft equipped with a rocket engine?"

"We use a plasma propulsion engine... the heat given off by the decay of radioactive material in our miniature thermal generator produces electricity, and the electric field thereof, heats and accelerates hydrogen ionizing it into a plasma; subjected to magnetic fields the highly conductive plasma is routed and ejected from the engine in the appropriate direction, creating varying degrees of thrust. We have thrusters positioned throughout the spacecraft."

"Your innovation intrigues me Click, Click, Buzz. What other technological inventions have you equipped to this space-age wonder?"

"This may be a source of fascination to you, Dr Barrett. We devised a means to overcome what is akin to osteoporosis, muscle atrophy and other such negative effects of weightlessness in outer space."

"That had crossed my mind, do reassure me."

"With pleasure… We have installed a vacuum chamber, similar to a Tokamak found on Earth, which utilises magnetic fields to confine the hydrogen plasma which you can infer has a dual purpose. We are very resourceful. Through the decay of the hydrogen plasma positrons are released, which are essential antimatter particles for our artificial gravity design. This chamber is located at the ceiling of our spaceship, and of course the floor is composed of ordinary matter. We worked on the assumption that antimatter exists in an inverted spacetime, exhibiting a positive mass, but with an intrinsic negative gravitational mass, causing a repulsive gravitational force between the roof and the floor, effectively pulling us downwards. Our entire hull of the spacecraft is a gravitational conducting shell."

"Remarkable."

The spacecraft effortlessly took off as looked out upon the Earth gradually receding into the distance. I could easily discern the cities from the multitude of lights – a beacon indicating life to a passer-by functioning at its own neurotic pace and purpose.

"Click, Click, Buzz, where is the wormhole located?"

"Thanks to that informative documentary, close to the planet with the most extensive ring system, which you refer to as Saturn."

"That is a mere seven hundred million odd miles. How did you find Earth?"

"On our arrival, we presumed the astronomical model for your solar system is heliocentric and that there is the potential for a planet to be in the habitual zone. We embarked on a journey to the sun eliminating each planet along the way. We approached Saturn but did not dare get any closer due to the hazardous ring particles. We orbited Jupiter performing orbit trim manoeuvres when necessary but abandoned our approach due to high pressure. We landed on Mars, but we determined from our sensory equipment that the composition of the atmosphere is mainly carbon dioxide and very little trace of oxygen, eventually causing hypoxia. At last, we came across Earth, and of course, discovered life." "Fascinating. Click, Click, Buzz, you are adept at spatial orientation and are quite the skilled pilot, it's a travesty to deny me the knowledge of a technological demonstration of this wonderous machine of innovation."

"I appreciate your appraisal, as before, I don't see why our two civilisations can't share our collective knowledge, approach the command module and take the helm – keep her straight and true. There are two manoeuvres I will teach you, trajectory correction for minor flight-path amendment and in the event that we are not presented with the opportunity of a gravity-assist flyby, we will perform a deep space manoeuvre. Precision is key here Dr Barrett."

"Can you let me fly through the asteroid belt between Mars and Jupiter?"

"To my embarrassment, I myself was not capable of that, I had to surrender the controls to Click, Click, Buzz, Zing who is a far more accomplished pilot."

"I think I am a natural."

"That's excessive Dr Barrett, we have yet to deviate from our trajectory, and with that we will bring to an end the lesson."

"Just a while longer."

"We will all take rotating shifts at piloting. I of course will observe you, but in the intermittent period, I propose you adopt our practice of meditating interspersed with sleep."

"You seek nirvana?"

"We seek communion with our divinities."

"I find it hard to believe your civilisation is infested with superstition."

I sat and stared in disbelief at Click, Click, Buzz, Zing as he quietly convened with the mythological beings. I was disappointed to find these intelligent creatures had conceived of a religion, my expectation, given the core integration of science into their culture, is that they would be a secularist civilisation without a system of false beliefs. I had to repudiate this subversive delusion.

"Click, Click, Buzz, why do you believe in the divinities?"

"In my native land, theological notions were prohibited, morality dispensed with for a more robust cause; we were taught than nothing is mightier than our civilisation, and shall anything oppose it, even if it were a miraculous intervention availing my kind, it will be met with the wrath of our military, as no interference is permitted. Deities are deprecated by our warriors; they cower in the shadows at our heroism, too fearful to reveal themselves, if they were to exist. Or at least that was what we were taught. Once I emigrated, my perspective altered on the night of the ritual initiation when the revelation occurred. Their voices spoke to me, captivating me with their wisdom. It was the most profound and prophetic experience I have had, and it gave me a fantastic insight into my scientific research."

"Were you inebriated?"

"To begin with it was an unusual induction; I smelt this beautiful aroma, became acutely euphoric and was instantly transported. I was told the entire entourage at the ritual was also affected and that it was normal practice for the deities to reveal themselves in such a manner."

"Have you ever considered that the voices and hallucinations were symptoms of a psychotic episode?"

"I cannot deny their existence and I wish to commune with them once more, but they are elusive deities, appearing only at an auspicious time. I shall reveal no more. Excuse me I must meditate as the shamans had advised."

Despite my admiration for the extent of his devotion, I would not partake in this preposterous activity, instead I would sleep, and spend my waking hours navigating the splendours of the universe. The Arachnids encouraged me to meditate but relented given my aversion to feigned worship, they left me to sleep, only waking me, with a gentle prod, when it was time for my lessons.

"Mesmerising, Click, Click, Buzz, is that Mars?"

"Yes, Dr Barrett. As planned, we have the opportunity for a gravitational slingshot altering our trajectory towards

Jupiter, exploiting the orbital energy. This is going to be extremely low altitude, approximately one hundred and fifty kilometres from the surface. Start the descent procedure."

"I am far from confident about this."

"Stern propellant. Starboard, Starboard."

"Okay, you're unnerving me... I can't remember is that right or left?"

"Right, Dr Barrett."

"Firing thrusters."

"Five second thrust on the bow and allow gravity do the rest, Dr Barrett. You will notice the magnitude of our velocity returns to roughly the same as our entry when we leave the gravitational pull, but relative to the sun we have gained significant momentum."

We coasted around Mars on a trajectory to Jupiter to repeat the process but first we had to overcome the asteroid belt.

"Wow, that is impenetrable."

"Marvel at Click, Click, Buzz, Zing's piloting."

I witnessed a virtuoso, he inched us through thrust by thrust. Whenever collision was imminent, he reacted with finesse, eluding disaster.

"Click, Click, Buzz, Zing, I have to say that was impressive."

"Nothing a rookie couldn't have done, with the exception of Click, Click, Buzz, of course."

"Must you continually single me out for criticism?"

"Bing, bing, gabbit, da."

"What did he say Click, Click, Buzz?"

"He is making fun of me."

"Classic."

Our journey had been perilous but rewarding. We were on course to reach Saturn.

"Look Dr Barrett, do you see it?"

"Yes, it looks like a giant bubble."

"That is the wormhole."

"Fascinating."

We entered. I braced myself. It certainly was a tunnel; the perpendicular view was a distortion of colours but when I looked in the longitudinal direction, I could distinctly see the Arachnids Galaxy. We emerged unscathed from the space warp and pressed on.

Without forewarning the aliens said that we were ten hours away from landing, but I had been psychologically preparing for this encounter, my speech had been memorised, delivering a message of peace. The spacecraft entered the alien atmosphere, approached swiftly, stopped suddenly and then hovered above ground, it then flew at an adjacent angle. As I was looking out the window at a luscious valley, Click, Click, Buzz, halted the space craft to a stationary position with the underside thruster burning. Click, Click, Buzz, Zing then began to talk into what looked like a walkie-talkie.

"We are announcing your arrival Dr Barrett. Rest assured you will have safe passage to your designated podium to address our kin."

The ramp opened, and I was greeted by armed arachnids. They escorted me into a hole in the ground which led to a steel doorway and into an underground compound. We took an elevator like contraption into the very bowels of the beast.

"Dr Barrett this is your room. Please get settled and we will summon you when the assembly begins."

"I would prefer to be outside in the fresh air."

"Sorry Dr Barrett but you must stay here. It is very tense out there."

"I had anticipated they would be fascinated by me."

"They're not impressed with your feeble stature, but I have warned them of your power."

With no reference to time, I impatiently waited, and waited, and waited. Although they did not renege on the agreement per se, too much time had passed without dialogue with the Arachnids. I could no longer dispute that I had been deceived and imprisoned, left to perish of dehydration and starvation, inhumane creatures you shall suffer at my hands. All I had to do was locate and possess a nearby Arachnid but there didn't appear to be anyone in close proximity, they knew the extent of my hyperphysicality and clearly left the area unmanned. But what they failed to realise is that I can break this door down with my telekinesis. I thrust my arms out, holding them straight towards the door, concentrating as much force as I could and unleashed it, but there was no impact, as a matter of fact nothing happened. I repeated the action over and over, but it proved ineffective. I had to get a run at the door I thought, I went to the very back of the room and sprinted towards it, hoping that the kinetic energy would trigger my telekinesis, upon collision I bounced off, left sprawled out on the floor in great pain. Despondent and exhausted from my exertions, I curled up into a ball and slept.

I awoke, looked towards the door, in a half-dazed state, I pointed my finger towards it and confounded thing flew open. That's a pleasing illusion, which I instantly dismissed as a hallucination caused through my malnourished state. I paced around the cell wallowing in despair and castigating myself for being a servile fool; for not applying my trusted cynicism to these infernal creatures. Incarceration is not sufficient punishment for my stupidity, I must inflict self-harm to fully understand the error of my way. I banged my head off the wall repeatedly until I drew blood, whilst shouting abuse at myself. After all the commotion, regret permeated though my being for abstaining from the instigation of my plan upon arrival. During all of this I kept impulsively and repeatedly glancing at the doorway, it appeared to remain unimpeded with the door unhinged on the ground. My scepticism waning, I walked over to it to give it a tap, but there was no surface to make contact. The door was indubitably on the floor.

In disbelief I walked out of the room and began searching the other rooms to conform my suspicions – it had been completely vacated. I came across an elevator but was operated by a biometric fingerprint scanner. I had been foiled once more. I sat and waited next to the elevator for any activity, no such luck. I became frustrated by this, conjured my telekinesis, ruptured the elevator door, walked in and without any hand gestures, I looked at the ceiling panel of the elevator and imagined it blowing open, to which it did with great force that the entire contraption shook. I hoisted myself through the opening, climbed the cable to the floor above and prised the elevator door open. I was confronted by armed Arachnids who upon seeing me hesitated in disbelief. I was amused at their inferiority and possessed them all in one fell swoop. I took refuge in a room whilst looking through the eyes of Click, Click, Buzz's comrades. Any alien with a gun will inadvertently become my ally, the rest were expendable, forming a line I despatched of them with a laser to the back of the head at point blank range just to be sure. I took a laser gun from an Arachnid and identified from the dead bodies who I considered to be the highest rank – I had very little to go on. I pulled its arms from its mosaic sac, aimed the laser gun at the knuckle joint and surgically removed the finger which I put in my pocket. Given the capacity of the elevator and the number of Arachnids I had at my disposal it took a few journeys to get everyone to the floor above. Of course, by this time we had drawn attention to ourselves, but before any resistance was prompted, I manipulated a soldier, moving him into other rooms, all the while seeing through his eyes, as with the previous floor only the armed conscript's lives were spared. After repeating the process for two more floors I had finally reached the fortifying entrance.

I thought the best strategy would be to blitz them with the element of surprise weakening their resolve. I had all my comrades charge out of the hole but when I saw through their eyes, I could see soldiers lined up around the circumference of the hole who unleashed a barrage of lasers wiping out my first battalion. I rushed again with a squadron hoping that at least one could survive in time for me to possess those on the ground, which he did. The opposing faction could no longer identify a friendly from a foe, I myself had trouble discerning who was the enemy so I had my conscripts fire indiscriminately in all directions. The unpossessed reluctantly returned fire in a desperate attempt to neutralise the rogue assailants, some were unwilling to shoot their own kind and fled the scene. With a solitary Arachnid, I took a step back from the battle to assess who had the advantage but all I could observe was total confusion, lasers permeating through the blood and guts, bodies mangled on the ground and shrill screeches echoing in the valley. I surveyed the surrounding area and noticed an encampment of Arachnids on the cusp of the valley. I tactfully had them join the battle which erupted into full scale war. In amongst all this bloodshed and perplexity there was a real precision killer, he was a warrior, he must have killed fifty of those beasts single handily. For some reason I imagined this to be Click, Click, Buzz, Zing so I assembled a large task force to capture him and bring him back to the compound. I felt he deserved this treatment given his valour. When he arrived at the entrance, I possessed him, opened the door, and moved him in to the room that I had commandeered.

"Hello Click, Click, Buzz, Zing."

"Ethan, release me you confounded fool. I had to slay my kin because of you and now they're all shooting at each other. I am in a state of utter disbelief… I will kill you for this."

"Enough, I have to mastermind a war."

Once I felt assured of my victory, I ceased the gunfire, and clambered through the hole in the ground accompanied Click, Click, Buzz, Zing. There were bodies everywhere, massacred. I had a total of approximately one hundred and thirty conscript's leftover. They all looked shocked by what had happened. Some were inconsolable. Most likely because they had slaughtered their comrades in a merciless battle.

"Okay, Dr Barrett, the situation can still be rectified. Please just cease all transgressions."

"We are past the point of no return, Click, Click, Buzz, Zing. You betrayed me, left me to die in a prison."

"Had you demonstrated restraint and patience in this delicate matter you would have understood the preparation required until we felt assured of our safety."

"That is a deceptive notion you are expounding. I shall not retreat; humanity has won the war."

"You call this a war Dr Barrett? This was just a minor precaution. We will annihilate you. Wait for the bombs."

"Ah, as anticipated your countermeasure – a feeble nuclear arsenal. I am correct in presuming that they are monitoring the area?"

"With spacecrafts…"

"I can't fathom why you are foolishly divulging such information."

"You are going to be killed, Ethan, no matter what I say."

"Okay, follow me, Click, Click, Buzz, Zing, we are going back in the bunker."

"Aren't you going to fight the war?"

"I will, but not with these hands."

Back underground I felt safe again. Click, Click, Buzz, Zing was saddened and infuriated about what he had seen, and I think he began to realise the mistake he had made by informing me of the incoming threat, but he still couldn't comprehend what I could do from this bunker.

I had my army move upon the land, growing in stature, as I possessed what I could and terminated all others within my path. We spread fast and swift like an unstoppable virus infecting all within reach. This was mass genocide, and it was taking place at my command, innocent aliens who, as far as I know, had not harmed anyone despite their perceived intentions towards me. I foresee a future of remorse for my actions. But I couldn't help but enjoy my position of the general leading my army against the alien scum, destroying them in one strategic move, and what a move it was. As my army continued to descend upon the land, suddenly I felt a tremor, the whole bunker shook.

"Your comrades are certainly not averse to a little excessive force."

"I consider it to be a commensurate response to the threat humanity pose."

"That's rather flattering but will act with circumspection, let's move to a lower level."

I apprehensively anticipated a strategic retaliation with Click, Click, Buzz's invention equipped that would sway the balance of the war. It was no less apocalyptic when the spacecraft descended, in an aerial bombardment firing a barrage of lasers at my division but to my surprise they were visible. To further compound the inherent weakness of the design of the spacecraft, although aerodynamic, they were better adapted to deep space travel and the trajectory was predictable from the expulsion of fumes from the thrusters, not even Click, Click Buzz's ingenuity could overcome this fatal flaw. I quickly adopted deflection shooting, to the harrowing realisation of the pilots, who attempted to deceive me with a quick short burst in one direction and then a long-sustained burst in the opposite direction; their erratic movements affected the accuracy of their lasers, but the sheer mass surpassed the firepower of my army, I resorted to retreating my conscripts to a nearby forest to take cover. A cluster soon formed of spacecraft concentrating their fire power into the trees, decimating the poor foliage, I focused all my energy into one Arachnid, fixated onto the stagnant adversaries in the air, locked on to them and as I moved my head they did to, until I brought them down to the ground in a fiery explosion. The skies fell silent, the tension was palpable. To my surprise, the Arachnids had not forgone their assault on land; a dark spec on the horizon got larger and larger as an army of arachnids began to bear down on my meagre battalion, the fools. Provided with this leverage I set about possessing them. Soon a large portion broke rank and turned on their emissaries. But this was nothing more than a diversion tactic, a new formation of spacecraft appeared but this time dispersed with quicker and more erratic movements making it difficult to apprehend them, it was an absolute necessity for me to commander their spacecraft and meet them head on. The spacecraft, distracted by the main battle, gave me an opportunity to sneak a small covert group out the periphery to scour the area for some advantage. What ensued was the stalking, at a distance, of a cowardly Arachnid who deserted his comrades and made a brake for it. The unsuspecting dope led me straight to an airfield where there was an abundance of spacecrafts. I possessed all the arachnids that were guarding it and had them operate the spacecrafts to counter the aerial threat.

I terrorized the skies, sacrificing a portion of my escadrille in a frontal assault while I flanked the Arachnids from the rear obliterating them. Dogfighting tactics proved effective, the absence of fear or potential death was crucial in engagement with the enemy, it gave me the upper hand. Anarchy reigned as they evaded direct conflict and retreated. I chased and harried them, obliterating those I could. I inferred from their haphazard manoeuvres that they had the intention of taking shelter on land but were reluctant to give away any sites of strategic importance. With no other alternative than to regroup, the Arachnids put up a defensive front in a cubic formation facing all directions with the exception of down to the ground. As a decoy I surrounded their structure with the intent to intimidate them into an ill-advised attack, whilst ambushing them from below. Again, they dispersed in all directions as I gave chase. The protracted aerial battel raged on for what I assumed was years, but once I had nullified the threat, I directed my attention to their wooden boats in the ocean, they had no artillery and proved to be easy targets. I methodically set about eradicating any trace of the Arachnids civilisation from the planet, but I presumed they had more bunkers constructed underground and I devised a simple method of amassing a giant search party of conscripts, on foot and in the air, to ascertain where these bunkers were. Over the course of the search, I came across many each accessible through an aperture in the ground and protected by a solid door. I imagined myself passing through the entryway, and I could see the door from the opposite side through the eyes of an Arachnid. I had him walk to the door and raise the obstruction. I took each bunker by force, preventing any attempt at retaliation. At one such site, I discovered a missile silo containing nuclear war heads. This may appear as a useful expedient, but it would remain as a last resort since contamination of any area of this world with radiation is to be avoided. Only the valley that I am in would be condemned.

I came across all types of new species on the war path, but it was one in particular that wreaked havoc on my army. They were a cat like species which seemed to fear the arachnids but, on some occasions, they mustered the courage and attacked. My army was so large that the few that perished were mere collateral damage, but I had to break formation every time which disrupted my offensive. Given these attacks I had to be vigilante after all I controlled this army. Having accumulated at my command a few billion conscripts, I hunted and flushed out most of the cat like creatures to prevent attack on my human colony, which proved to be difficult as they are elusive beasts, along with solitary groups of Arachnids, killing them all.

When I slept in an isolated room from Click, Click, Buzz, Zing, it gave Arachnids the opportunity of a counter strike, but on each occasion, they failed to exact retribution as their army lay in disarray. By this time, my bunker had been hit numerous times by nuclear bombs as the bunker shock with great intensity. Fortunately, they hadn't been able to penetrate deep underground and I remained safe. I knew from these attacks that there must be one missile silo remaining, but I couldn't find it. Why they hadn't utilised nuclear bombs against the rogue assailants I am not sure, perhaps they were unable to bring themselves to kill too many of their own flesh and blood. Or perhaps it was because they couldn't ascertain who's on their side and who's not. Poor aliens. The aerial search expanded to mountain ranges, scanning all along the periphery. It proved fruitful as I discovered tracks up the mountains which lead to bunkers as before I passed into the bunker, possessed the conscripts, and had them join the ranks of my army. Several weeks passed without any tremors so I concluded I had taken control of them all. Having been satisfied that I had eradicated any trace of these beasts, the spacecrafts alighted, and the pilots vacated their cockpits and joined the horde. I had the portion of arachnids with laser guns to start killing the ones without. There was a mass that remained, armed and dangerous, so the final act of atrocity I would commit was to have the remaining conscripts commit suicide in the most painless way possible - a laser to the head. There were bodies lying everywhere, piled up in fact.

I could ascertain that many years had passed in which I committed the most heinous war crimes, killed an entire civilisation, and took an entire planet as my own. Click, Click, Buzz, Zing failed to truly apprehend this from inside of the bunker and chose to humour himself with my exploits, but I informed him thus once more.

"And that brings an end to the military campaign; the strategic resolution of the conflict fulfilled."

"Bravo Dr Barrett, you have exceeded all expectations by cowering in this bunker."

"You saw what I did to your comrades on the surface, they inexplicably shot at each other."

"Our capabilities far exceed your sorcery."

"You must be referring to your ineffective nuclear bombs, spritely spacecraft and horde of an army. Perhaps I'm not giving your civilisation enough credit, I applaud your instruments of war, comparable in many ways to that of humanity. Travelling through the wormhole, ingenious. But isn't it ironic that I turned your strengths into weakness, that is the true art of war."

"You have hidden in here like a quivering coward."

"I have not quivered you beast. I have brought your species to extinction."

"Ethan, I am not properly equipped to stage an intervention of this nature, so I will inform you thus, you are delusional."

"Given that comprehension of the great spectacle is unattainable without observation, I will excuse your naivety, but if you maintain this denial, I will have to castigate you for being an ignorant creature."

"Dr Barrett, you have overestimated your power and deluded yourself in the process, it is physically impossible for you to control the entire population of my kind; let alone from three levels underground."

"You witnessed me control your comrades from one level underground, why not three?"

"I have grown weary of this Ethan. Our chiefs will have realised that the nuclear bombs haven't penetrated the bunker and will send an army to kill you. They are just biding their time."

"Poor ill-informed Arachnid, your comrades are dead, they will not liberate you from this tomb nor put an end to my reign of terror. You have exceeded your usefulness and now must be killed to put an end to your kind. I am saddened by this given our acquaintance over the course of the past few years. I have come to see you as more of a friend than a foe."

"I have enjoyed your commentary of the great war as you call it... Lets allow friendship to prevail Dr Barrett, we can come to a resolution, and neither party should have to compromise. Follow me Dr Barrett."

Curious to know what he was plotting I released him.

"Dr Barrett, I am an ally at this stage, do remember I directed you to where the food and water are stored."

"Yes, there was an abundance, enough to sustain the populace of this bunker for many years to come. Without it I would have never survived, and I thank you for that."

"What are friends for? Dr Barrett. This room is where we store the hazmat suits."

"I must commend your civilisation for the preparation for interplanetary warfare. It appears your entire infrastructure and philosophy have been predicated on war with an alien species."

"It is the only conceivable threat, Dr Barrett. We would only be destroying our deepest essence, the unprejudiced reflection of the self, had civil war broke out, and we all understood this as much."

"That's a rather insipid attitude, no wonder I won the war."

"Of course, you did. Take this Dr Barrett."

"I presume this suit is to protect me from the radiation…? I don't think it would be prudent of me to leave the bunker with you."

"I can cease all hostilities when we reach the surface; if you are willing to surrender to the chiefs, but don't become disillusioned by this, it will merely be a pretence to appease them of course, you don't have to forgo your delusion of power."

"How dare you! I will destroy you, impudent beast!"

And with that I picked up a laser gun and executed him. It occurred to me that a cremation ceremony involving Click, Click Buzz, Zing's carcass would be a symbolic consummation of the modus operandi of my campaign to eradicate the Arachnids; however, to commemorate their civilisation I dubbed this world 'Planet Arachne'. I hauled his lifeless body to the medical bay where I wrapped him up in sanitary clothing. I weakly succumbed to rolling a cigarette, which I had successfully resisted temptation of hitherto, to expurgate my subconscious of my misconduct. I too resolved to destroy any form of identification on my presence by placing my wallet and other belongings nestled in my pockets onto the makeshift pyre, as I had become a disparate figure with a corrupted self-perception, I could no longer associate the present with my past self. I, the radical embodiment of a demigod, immortalised in the culmination of my life's work, had been reduced to nothing more than mutated abomination, a monster. I castoff this depiction into the fiery abyss as I set fire to Click, Click, Buzz, Zing with my lighter and watched him burn. Smoke bellowed from the belly of the beast to the point where I had to leave the room.

This may appear contrary, but I could not jeopardise my health with the carcinogenic materials and radioisotopes from the fallout, so I struggled to get into the very large six-legged hazmat suit. I resorted to fitting my two legs in and then wrapping the rest around me. I had been confined to the third floor, necessitating the use of the elevator contraption. Neglecting the functionality, I prised open the door to find that it had collapsed onto the floor below. I looked up the shaft and could see daylight breaking through. I braced myself, once more unto the breach, I climbed up the vertical exterior, pushed my way through the soil and emerged in a huge crater. The entire first floor was penetrated by the blasts and visible from the top of the crater. I struggled through the ashy terrain and debris, with my visibility obscured by a dust cloud until I made it out the valley. I looked back upon the ravaged scenery condemned to a desolate wasteland. I acknowledge that this was war, but it evoked anger in me at their complete disregard for preserving the ecological habitat, dispensing with decency in favour of moral turpitude when confronted by their own mortality. I stood atop a mound and stared at the apocalyptic scene and allowed my visceral reaction to dissipate, poor aliens. The only fair interpretation of this conflict is that they are a desperate victim retaliating against an omnipotent miscreant. These creatures have been absolved by I, the measure of evil.

If only humanity had taken similar dooms day prepping measures for an alien invasion, adopting the very core principles of survivalism, I wouldn't have had to come to the rescue of my feeble race. At first a full-scale reconnaissance operation would be under way to scout for military bases, made feasible by Click, Click, Buzz's cloaking device, with the only apparent betrayal by the fumes from their thrusters, yet this would be imperceptible unless under close scrutiny. With a schematic of the battleground the coordinated two-pronged attack would have overwhelmed our disjointed and disorganised military, compelling the sovereign nations to mobilise aerial, naval and infantry forces; however, confronted by the sheer logistics of coordinating a global offensive, especially considering the brevity in which to act, would be a futile reprisal. The Arachnids would methodically despatch each strategic stronghold expeditiously, from aerial bombardment to armour encrusted beasts wielding laser guns, the sheer mass would have trampled our soldiers, demolished our tanks, evaded our missiles, denigrating humanity to hasher climates, scavenging resources undesirable to the Arachnids, or driven to extinction.

Before I departed, I wanted to locate a site in which to setup my colony, the perfect location was a particular bunker I ravaged with such ferocity I dismembered the unsuspecting victims; embedded high up the mountains given its remoteness and relative safeness from the remaining creatures although observably harmless to my colony I had to be cautious. I whipped off my hazmat suite, embarked on journey to a nearby airfield, boarded the spacecraft and took flight to our new settlement. On my arrival I was confronted by the steel entryway, I neglected my telekinesis and thus had no means to enter and no existent Arachnids within that I could possess to open the door. I had to adopt my contingency plan which was to scour the mountainous region extensively until my perseverance paid dividends. My methodical approach of eliminating one behemoth from another lead me to an observatory perched on the summit of an innocuous mountain, much like the one Click, Click, Buzz had described to me. I alighted the spacecraft on a precarious ledge, at the fortified entrance was a one of my old socks which I had abandoned in the spacecraft due to them being crusty and repugnant, this could be no mere coincidence.

Easily accessible given the reinforced steel door had been left open, I inspected the inside to discover no sign of violence or mutilated Arachnid bodies, which supported my recollection that I had never invaded this citadel on my conquest. I pried my way through the compound facility happening upon a docking bay with twelve spacecraft. To my astonishment, the other sock to my pair lay on a ramp of one of the spacecrafts. A trail of crumbs I thought, I must investigate. In front of me, was the cloaking device lever on the command module. That wily character, Click, Click, Buzz must have flown to this location after my imprisonment. This must have been his classified workshop, how intriguing. What occurred to me prior but was more evident is that Click, Click, Buzz's invention was still in the development stage, having not been applied to his comrades' spacecrafts. I had all the necessary accoutrements to return to Earth; a spacecraft with the cloaking device equipped to avoid detection, a coordinate system, and rations from the pantry of the bunker which I stocked the spacecraft with.

Chapter 6
A Fine Line

All at my disposal, a galactic coordinate system... Once I had ascended to space I could not for the life of me figure out my current longitude and latitude to extrapolate my position relative to the black hole. The apparently simple task of piloting to the exact degree measurement of angle relative to the sun, the galactic centre of the Arachnid's galaxy, galactic north pole and equator baffled me. I was despondent, and in a panic, I started to pace around the cockpit, cursing my luck. If I don't think of something, I am going to be stranded in this useless space-age contraption in a far-flung galaxy with no hope of returning to my select cadre. I looked at the screen of the command module once more, hoping to devise a solution, and right there, completely oblivious to me until now, was a little post-it note next to a button that read 'Push me', how could I not have seen this? Those cunning Arachnids must have acquired it during my English tutoring. Concerned that when pressed an explosion would be detonated within the hull, I cautiously, lowered my finger, closer and closer, perspiring heavily, I clicked it.

"Hello Dr Barrett, Click, Click Buzz, here. Do not fear a reprisal on my part for I am talking to you posthumously, murdered in cold blood, of course. Lend me your ears you scoundrel, first of all, I am ashamed for stealing a pen and paper to show my comrades these counterproductive but fascinating items, but that's a minor infraction. What is of greater importance is that after you were escorted to your quarters the Elders revealed themselves to me prophesising your victory. I chose to become a martyr to their prediction. They too appealed to my faith that I should aid you in your return to Earth. Thus, I left you a trail to follow in the sheer chance you discovered it and reprogrammed the navigation system into English, and permitted you access to our beacon technology. All you have to do press this button again and say out loud the password, 'Dr Barrett', and you will be guided to our transmitter placed in the extremities of the wormhole and throughout the course to Earth, so you simply have to fly towards the flashing dot on the interface. In the realisation that war was inevitable and there had to be a victor, in awe of your indomitable power, I graciously accept defeat, wishing you the best of luck on your journey and harbour no feelings of ill will towards you. Perhaps in another life we could have co-existed peacefully as friends if the fate of our two civilisations hadn't depended on us."

It was a lonely and harrowing journey to the milky way relying heavily on the thrusters but thankfully uneventful. This could not be said for my native galaxy. I was too afraid to perform a gravity slingshot of Jupiter, opting instead for a hefty burn propelling me towards Mars where I had more courage to perform the tricky flyby assist. Before I can breathe a sigh of relief, I had to negotiate the asteroid belt. I evaded a cluster with a short thrust, inadvertently projecting me into the path of a giant asteroid. I thought this was it.

Killed by my own hubris. But I swung into action thrusting again and again bypassing the congested congregation of rock. By the time Earth appeared on the horizon I had brass cojones.

I descended towards the Kingdom itself, my trajectory was disrupted by the drag caused by air resistance, I had not practiced entering a planet's atmosphere at this speed, yet once it reached terminal velocity, I regained partial control. Hurtling towards Earth, praying to any deity that would heed my call, in desperation that the exterior is a sufficient resistant to this aerodynamic inferno… I judged that it was the optimal time to decelerate with my thrusters, I came to a steady hover above the ground before imminent death struck its cruel blow. Once again, I had determined my own fate and retained my impiety for I had no need for a godly intervention. Not far from the city I flew towards the lake where it all began, negotiated a tricky touchdown in the surrounding foliage, disembarked and fastened the ramp with the locking panel, discarding the spacecraft for the time being without much trepidation of being discovered, as even if one where to come into proximity of it, they would simply, walk into an invisible object. Uncomprehendingly they would hopefully disregard the whole experience and walk off. I made haste towards the city to make a surprise visit to my parents. Having burnt my possessions, I was left with no alternative than to hike for hours. I vigorously knocked on the door in excited anticipation to see my parents who I missed dearly. The matriarch herself, who raised me into the man I am today, opened the door and upon sight of me fainted.

"Gwendoline are you okay?"

"What are you an apparition? Come to visit me from beyond the grave?"

"No Gwendoline it is I, your son, Ethan, I have returned."

"It can't be, you died many years ago. I buried you."

"For an obvious reason that is impossible."

"I must confess your body wasn't recovered but we did place sentimental items in your grave. Are you a ghost? Oh no, perhaps a demon? I should call Reverend Duguid to perform an exorcism."

"What on earth are you talking about? Let me put this in terms you will understand. I am still alive, occupational stress and failure of my ambitions led me to emigrate to California to escape ridicule from the scientific institution I was employed at reaching the public domain in some sort of smear campaign, and not to mention the vast debt they incurred at my behest. I thought if I disappeared all would be forgotten."

"Is that why Dr Scholtz some years ago tied up your father and I and threatened to harm us if we didn't tell him where you are?"

"Partly, yes but don't worry Dr Scholtz got his comeuppance in the end."

"I'm glad to hear it. Why did you not tell us you were leaving?"

"I was too ashamed to face you."

"Your own mother? You know I obliged to have unconditional love for you."

"Anyway Gwendoline, where is Ian?"

"Oh Ethan, Ian passed away some time ago from prostate cancer."

"I am sorry I wasn't there to support you through the emotional torment of bereavement."

"I survived Ethan, but my heart yearned for you both every hour of the day."

"May I stay here for a few weeks I need to get my affairs in order."

"Of course, my dear, I am going to need a moment to come to terms with your sudden appearance and miraculous resurrection."

"Okay I will go to my room. As soon as you have apprehended that I am alive, knock on the door and we can talk."

My mother and I became reacquainted, but I had the impression that she still believed I was spectre conjured up to haunt her – never mind at least I am providing her with companionship. With insurance cover in place to drive my mother's car and my allowance - she inherited my wealth as per my will and testament, and with power of attorney became wildly autocratic drip feeding me my savings.

"What use does a demon have of material possessions?"

"Power I suppose… Gwendoline for goodness' sake, I want you to schedule an appointment with your solicitor next week to resolves this farce."

"If you promise not to banish my pure soul to eternal damnation."

"First of all, that's a fallacy of a belief and secondly I am not the devil Gwendoline."

After convincing my mother that my intentions with her car were not nefarious, I set off for the university with a shifting stream of consciousness to impose upon Dr Wilde. I went straight to his office and knocked. I did wonder if he had maintained his position after all these years in this institute for learning.

"Do let yourself in. I am currently indisposed with my life's work."

"Hello, Dr Wilde. Your enthusiasm and dedication have not diminished since we last spoke."

"It can't be... you're dead ... I was at your funeral."

"I am alive and well, Dr Wilde."

"What was with the disappearing act?"

"Occupational hazard."

"And the only alternative was to vanish?"

"I reluctantly betray my heroism and admit that I am a coward who took flight, exiling myself in a foreign land."

Dr Wilde apprehended my sudden appearance judiciously and with sensitivity. I proceeded to deceive Dr Wilde about my emigration in the same manner as my mother and abruptly brought the conversation to the purpose of my visit.

"Dr Wilde, I have a favour to ask... If you could be so kind and grant me a lecture with some of your esteemed colleagues, I would be ever so grateful?"

"By all means. I am sure if it is not informative it will be entertaining."

"Certainly will, Dr Wilde."

"Do you care to share with me the subject matter?"

"I can give you a title... Colonialism on Planet Arachne."

"Oh, intriguing."

"You seem disappointed."

"I just occurred to me that this may reflect badly upon me."

"Don't worry Dr Wilde I shall not embarrass you."

"I know Dr Barrett; I am just winding you up old chum. It's good to have you back. So, things didn't work out with you and Dr Scholtz, that's a shame I thought that would be a good career move for you. Did you know just like you he disappeared some time ago?"

"No, I didn't."

"Yes, very mysterious... I thought you had run off together and eloped."

"And I trust that you wanted to be ordained to officiate the wedding?"

"Quite so, I was devasted when no invitation arrived."

"Sorry to disappoint, Dr Wilde. I will be sure to include you if marriage does materialise in the future."

"With that aside, do you realise it has been sixteen years since I last saw you? You must be in your mid-forties by now?"

"Yes, I am forty-six years old."

"My goodness, I am glad you experienced your youth in the vibrant city of San Francisco than stuck behind a desk with academic matters, this is one of my many regrets in life."

"Don't be ridiculous at least you have been productive and lived a life of value."

"I don't have much to show for it apart from a few peers approved papers in academic journals, no real recognition, I very much doubt I am next in line for the noble prize."

"Perhaps you should temper your ambition."

"I resigned myself to my fate a long time ago, to die in anonymity."

"That's rather tragic or perhaps melodramatic, Dr Wilde."

"On a cheerier note, you must be eligible for a green card in the land of opportunity, isn't that what all emigrants aspire to, a permanent residency? Surely your no different?"

"I must be eligible now, I never really enquired with the proper authorities. I no longer fit into the category of an immigrant though, as I have decided to settle in my native land."

"Very good, the Yanks don't compare to us barbarous Picts. Well, I am glad I have my friend at my beck and call again, and I do look forward to this lecture."

To my amazement the crowd were chanting my name and cheering.

"Dr Barrett! Dr Barrett!"

"Was this your handiwork Dr Wilde?"

"I may have told them to give you a rousing reception. No pressure. Ladies and gentlemen, I give you the legendary Dr Barrett."

Emboldened by the atmosphere and energy in the room, I addressed the assembly.

"Thank you for the standing ovation. Please be seated. The sensationalism of what I am about to tell you will ripple on to future generations for the duration of humanities transitory existence. Suspend your disbelief temporarily for what I am about to say… I have met two intelligent extra-terrestrials through a chance encounter, they were scouting earth for a habitable planet, I taught them English and befriended them. The dynamics of our friendship were plagued by cynicism, with the stakes so high we took to outwitting each other until at last trust was forged. Their names, Click, Click, Buzz and Click, Click, Buzz, Zing, are as strange as their appearance but they are affable creatures with a slight naivety. I took advantage of this to initiate a grand conquest on behalf of humanity, accompanying the aliens back their home planet, where a great battle ensued due to my imprisonment and the disillusion of my brotherly bond with the two creatures came to afore as a result of our allegiance to each of our own races. Had I not intervened the Arachnids, as I have denominated them, would have launched a pre-emptive strike upon earth eradicating humanity. I was left with no alternative than to reduce their civilisation to ash and bone, in doing so, commandeer a new world for humanity to colonise; it is rich and fertile, but more importantly, the chemical composition of the atmosphere is conducive to the sustainment of earthly life, such as ourselves. I stand before you, requesting you to join me on an interstellar journey to Planet Arachne to establish a colony."

"I am waiting for the punch line… This a stand-up sketch to incite laughter, isn't it? I couldn't imagine this to be serious."

"Well, it missed the mark in my opinion."

"Yes, it's not funny at all."

"Please refrain from airing any intrusive remarks whilst Dr Barrett is talking. Thank you."

"The immortal aim of humanity is implicit in our undertakings but is at the mercy of the economy of desire. Exploitation of the environment to satiate our veracious appetite for finite raw materials is triggering an ecological recession and climate change endangering the existence of all inhabitants on earth. The sole species with the capacity to comprehend and forecast the long-term consequences of its impact on nature, happens to be the most invasive, remaining impervious to the danger opting to dispense with the ominous overtones that threatens its comfortable existence, favouring a ponderous and inadequate response under the impression that this cyclical event will not lead to the extinction of mankind. By our very nature we are the architects of our own demise, but I have a solution that may preserve our world and populate anew. If you are incapable of inferring what I mean by this, then maybe you should stay behind... So, who will join me?"

The room fell silent, not even a whisper. A long and excruciating amount of time passed.

"No one? This is the opportunity of a lifetime?"

To which no one replied. To my shock and dismay, they started filing out of the lecture theatre without even acknowledging me, chattering amongst themselves about unrelated drivel. I couldn't believe it. When the last morsel had left the room, Dr Wilde looked at me with a frown about to rebuke me.

"Before you begin Dr Wilde, I am as perplexed as you are. I should have resorted to hyperphysically coercing them, why I gave them a chance to come on their own volition, I don't know. These people don't know what is good for them nor have the capacity to make a sound judgement for themselves. None of them are worthy of what I could have gifted them. They deserve to be abandoned to their sultry dominion to perish."

"Is that so Dr Barrett... Follow me to my office."

Dr Wilde escorted me there with a firm grip of my elbow.

"Please take a seat. I have a few phone calls to make."

He exited the room. I could hear an inaudible chatter coming from outside. I sat in bewilderment that what I said hadn't convinced them. My speech itself may have been brief but I certainly didn't lack conviction and the content alone should have compelled them enough.

I glanced at my watch, and with a double take I noticed an hour had passed. I attempted to open the door.

"Dr Wilde, why are you holding onto the handle and preventing me from leaving?"

"It's for your own safety. Trust me, you will thank me later."

"Hello Dr Barrett, this is constable MacGill accompanied by constable MacLerie. Please step away from the door."

"Okay, I am backing away."

Dr Wilde and two police officers entered the room.

"Ethan, Ethan Barrett?"

"Yes."

"You have been detained under the mental health act. We will escort you to Gartnavel hospital, please don't not resist or we will be left with no choice than to use force."

"Why have you done this Dr Wilde? I am not mentally ill. What I said is no mere invention of the mind, it is a literal empirical fact, you must believe me."
"I had to be objective about this Dr Barrett, following your unannounced emigration, or should I say sudden disappearance, and then that borderline deranged speech, I decided what is best for you is to involve the authorities. I phoned your mother; your next of kin and explained the situation. I didn't take much to persuade her, she agreed this was the right course of action."

"She's the one who needs a psychiatric evaluation, she thinks I am the devil, of course she will agree to my incarceration."

"I am trying to help you. You need help."

The constables took me by the arms. If I began to control one, out of necessity I would have to control them all. I would be exposed to the very organisation that I was trying to avoid... Against my better judgement I possessed the police officers, had them release me and walk a few feet away.

"What a paranormal occurrence... something has affected my cerebral cortex; I seem to have lost all control of my limbs, yet I still have sensation."

"MacLerie, it could be an incapacitating agent. It may be a terrorist plot; we should radio in reinforcements."

"What ideology do you think there are affiliated with MacGill?"

"I don't know but it is our duty to find out, and to neutralise them."

I was displeased with the association to the depraved indoctrinated recruits of these fanatical theologians but irrespective of this I could not possess the police officers indefinitely, reluctantly releasing them.

"Secure the parameter, MacLerie. Dr Barrett and Dr Wilde please take cover under the desk for your own safety."

Dr Wilde and I both looked at each other as if they were mad but complied, they were police officers after all.

"Area secure, and there is nothing out of the ordinary, MacGill. I think we have to rule out terrorism as a cause."

"It's safe for you to come out now doctors."

"Okay MacGill, we have a duty to uphold we will discuss this anomaly later."

The two police officers transformed back into their role of escorting me to the hospital much to my indignation.

"What is with you people? Perhaps you should stay away from me for your own protection."

"Are you claiming to be the source of this, Ethan?"

"Yes, officer MacGill."

"Don't listen to him he's delusional."

"Some friend you are Dr Wilde."

"Come with us Ethan, you are in need of urgent care."

I considered implanting thoughts but lacked the motivation having been ostracized from the community I once held dear. I resigned myself to the fate they had instore for me. They had no comprehension of what I had done for them, for future generations. This all seemed to fade into the abyss. I was insane to them; a raving, dishonourable lunatic detained and disgraced; off to a mental institution, to correct and debase.

The police officers lead me in through the automatic door where I noticed the loonies having visitation hours with their relatives in the reception area, from there we ascended a small ramp into a narrow corridor made a left at the next hallway, where a nurse greeted us at the security door. I was then led into an ominous room in the sanatorium where four people were sitting. They sat me down.

"We will take over from here, thank you."

The two police officers excused themselves and left.

"What if it was him MacGill?"

"Don't be ridiculous MacLerie, he's a nutcase."

"I heard that."

"Good evening, Ethan, my name is Dr Blake, and I am the psychiatrist at this fine institute. We are joined by my colleagues, Dr Easton, and Dr Anand who I will consult with in order to determine an appropriate treatment plan. Also here is an independent health advocate, Henry Dillinger who will explain your rights and options. Please discuss any issues you may have in detail with Henry. Now Ethan, you have been detained under section two of the mental health act. The duration for which you have been detained will be twenty-eight days, this may be extended if required. As you are a serious risk, we have taken this measure to ensure your safety and the safety of others."

"My intention is not to inflict harm upon myself or others but to escape from this prison."

"You are not a criminal, Ethan, but a patient and your illness shall not be stigmatised. As for your confinement based upon your progress you will be given privileges such as leaving the grounds for half an hour for a walk and fresh air. Now, Ethan I have been led to believe that you harboured persecutory paranoid delusions causing you to abscond to America for many years to escape unfounded ridicule from your friends, colleagues, and family. However, irrational this appears I understand how powerful these imperceptible threats can be to someone in your condition. Do you care to enlighten me with your version of the events that took place?"

"You're implying that it was all in my mind?"

"Not at all Ethan. I am sure you had good reason to disappear for sixteen years."

"I did and what you have described, a trip across the Atlantic, doesn't do justice to where I have been."

"Planet Arachne I presume? Do you really believe you have discovered a new habitable world and have viable means of transportation to and from it? And that it was a reasonable decision to share this belief with a room full of scientists?"

"You have no idea what I am capable of, but I must admit it was an error in judgement to disclose this information in the manner that I did."

"So, there is some semblance of sense in you. Excuse my rudeness, I am just trying to help you come to terms with your illness. I will make one parting remark from our session, I am impressed that you survived this long by yourself."

I received three appetizing meals a day and had a daily scheduled appointment with Dr Blake at three o'clock. I quickly settled into life in the psychiatric ward witnessing newcomers running amok of the staff, the nurses took measures to subdue the patients with thinly veiled threats of the legality of their behaviour, and if they resisted, a strong sedative would be administered into their buttocks. I took greater attention in monitoring the routine of the nurses to ascertain an optimum time to make a run for it. I hatched a plan to escape. I lingered close to the door trying not to draw attention to myself and witnessed a nurse type in the code to the locking mechanism, 'two-nine-three-eight-four'. I waited for the nurse to vacate the area, configured the code, and bolted. With my mother's credit card still within my possession I booked a night a hotel in George square as it was dark, and I didn't have the grit for a night in the cold. I woke up to a knock on the door.

"Officer MacGill, MacLerie, what are you doing here?"

"You're a lousy fugitive, Ethan. We will be escorting you back to the hospital."

"Wait MacGill, you said you would give me some time to interrogate him?"

"Very well MacLerie, I will be waiting outside the door."

"Take a seat, Ethan."

"Are you comfortable?"

"Yes. Ouch why did you punch me?"

"Reveal your secret, sorcerer."

"Stop hitting me. Is that a taser?"

"Only eighteen hours of training and I have already defeated you, you pathetic conjurer of black magic. I'm going to shock you to death unless you give me your power."

"Don't point that thing at me. Ahh!"

"I have to say I am getting enjoyment from watching you convulse on the floor."

I had to act quickly and implanted a thought into MacLerie's sadistic mind.

"I will not harm Ethan Barrett and return him to the hospital. He is not a sorcerer but an ordinary man."

"What the hell? Is that your pathetic attempt to get into my mind?"

For a brief moment I feared the man and since I couldn't harm him without facing the wrath of the law, I resorted to my newly devised technique of learning – the rote method. I transmitted the thought again repeatedly for approximately ten minutes, I could see the thought flashing through his mind as he started to rock back and forth in a trance like state, drool dripped from his mouth, his eyes glazed over and rolled back into his head, but I didn't cease until MacGill entered the room whereby I immediately desisted.

"Are you okay MacLerie?"

He remained silent in a comatose state.

"What have you done to him?"

"Nothing, he punched me a few times and then threatened to kill me and then went completely silent."

MacGill walked over to MacLerie and slapped him on the face.

"Snap out of it."

"Sorry MacGill I don't know what came over me. We better take this reprobate back to the loony bin."

"I will let it be known MacLerie I will not be writing a favourable report."

MacLerie's eyes frowned and locked onto mine, a blank look came on his face, and he shrugged it off. Whilst I was been escorted to the police car, I had a moment alone with MacGill.

"You traced my mother's credit card, that's how you found me. Admit it officer MacGill."

"Trade secrets, Ethan."

Back in relative safety away from the malevolent MacLerie, MacGill, handed me over to Dr Blake's care, where he rules with an instant prescription to treat all ailments.

"I am disappointed that you attempted to escape, I thought with your level of intellect you would realise we are here to help. I think that each action should incur a similar reaction but at this time I will adjourn any punishment until we have further assessed your cooperation so no retrospective action will be taken if you comply. Now to my psychiatric evaluation, the diagnosis. I think you are suffering from an acute psychotic episode which may be the result of an underlying schizophrenic illness. For this infliction I will prescribe fifteen milligrams of Olanzapine, which is a second-generation anti-psychotic medication which should help you manage your symptoms."

"I strongly disagree with this assessment and categorically refuse to take it."

An hour-long argument ensued until I eventually conceded and conformed with his demands. As a result of this cure I developed extrapyramidal side effects, so I was prescribed Cogentin to elevate my skin from crawling and muscles from spasming, and also Zopiclone for sleep deprivation. Dr Blake wasn't finished there, dispensing Diazepam due to irritability and Fluoxetine due to what he described as psychotic depression. The first two weeks under the influence of this concoction I was incoherent, drowsy, and lethargic but soon I began to feel better, not an elevated mood accompanied with insightful sagacious luminosity like Dr Schultz's wonder drug but definitely better, and with my confessions during his therapy sessions I began to doubt that Planet Arachne existed; that the spacecraft was a figment of my imagination, that Click, Click, Buzz was an imaginary acquaintance. I almost plucked up the courage to tell him that I was a serial killer, but I refrained.

"Have you had any patients believe they have telepathy?"

"Yes, Ethan, thought broadcasting is a common paranormal belief amongst schizophrenics."

"But what if people were reacting to what I thought?"

"A hallucination Ethan. Your chemically imbalanced brain is affecting your faculties, and you are being convinced by your own fantasies."

"From this day I shall never try it again."

"Good lad Ethan, we are making progress."

"Reiterate why the Arachnids don't exist?"

"The belief that aliens exist is one thing but to have met them and been abducted is an altogether separate matter, a delusion, Ethan."

"Hmm… How do you explain the fact that I have no recollection of the events that took place in America?"

"Your memories have been distorted and repressed upon your return and replaced by an alternate reality. What you believe to have happened is an illusion that you created to comfort yourself, dispensing with an incongruous reality that would abolish what remains of your diminished ego, this is further evidential in that you compensate for your inferiority complex with a coping mechanism of attributing yourself with superpowers as a result of sustained internal paranoia and persecution. Consequently, you have a strong resistance to realism; that existence is independent of your perception, which effectively constitutes your psychological construct of telepathy. In addition to this the infamy you attribute to yourself from the fictitious recollections of your past, is revealing, and perhaps indicative of a perverted self-perception correlating with an identity disturbance for I don't consider you to have the constitution for evil acts; with the inclusion of the profound delusion of mass genocide that causes you the most remorse and provocation of self-loathing. I believe these are all convoluted symptoms of your paranoid schizophrenia."

"That's a brutal assessment, Dr Blake... How did I survive without a job?"

"The truth hurts, Ethan. I am inclined to think that you had an occupation or else a visa would not have been granted. I have to work with you to uncover the truth which is buried somewhere deep in your unconscious. You seem capable of expressing actualities from the fragments of your past without realisation that you are doing it. Extraction through methods such as catharsis, psychodynamic and cognitive therapies, and reinforcement of these techniques through conscious acknowledgement will aid you to attain your true self rather than a phantom."

"I am committed to your treatment programme. I want to return to a former state of lucidity – I am quite lost due to overwhelming doubt."

Over the course of our session's Dr Blake convinced me that I should disassociate myself with my past events allowing his psychoanalytic interpretations to influence my retrospection and also to address the correlated delusions with hyperbolic doubt.

"How did I get schizophrenia?"

"I think it's hereditary, remaining latent until your formative years, as is the case in most circumstances, and exacerbated by the misuse of that experimental drug you told me about, which would better assist me if you could remember the name of it."

"Why do you think that was real but nothing else?"

"I don't doubt you were involved with narcotics; your character is very revealing."

On the twenty eighth day I was converted to the logic of Dr Blake, a disciple, utterly conditioned.

"Ethan, I have arranged for a taxi to take you back to your mother's house."

"Thank you, Dr Blake, for everything, you have brought me to my senses, purged any illogical beliefs from my mind."

"Pleasure Ethan. Do remember to setup up a repeat prescription at your local general practitioner, and I will see you for a follow up appointment at my office on Dumbarton Road in two weeks' time."

"I fully trust you and I am ready to tell you about my homicidal tendencies."

"What an inconvenience I just signed off for the day. It will have to wait until our scheduled appointment in two weeks' time, goodbye for now Ethan."

"Goodbye, Dr Blake."

"One hundred and ten Hyndland road, please."

"Sure thing."

With a shifting stream of consciousness.

"Hello, mother I'm home, open the door."

"Getaway or else I will phone the police."

"It's me, Ethan, your son."

"I had a son who was a distinguished scientist, you on the other hand are a disgrace, you are no son of mine but an evil imposter."

This transpired for quite some time until her threat was realised.

"Get away you archfiend. The police should be here any minute."

"Excuse me, Ethan Barrett."

"MacGill and MacLerie… Are there no other officers in the police force to deal with this?"

"Quite a coincidence, isn't it, Ethan?"

I fled the scene, sprinting at full pace with them hot on my heels. They chased me down to Byers Road where I was able to blend with the crowds and quickly dart down Great George Street to Kelvinbridge which I hid under. I waited, but they never appeared. Satisfied that I lost them, I set off for Dr Wilde's residence.

"Hello, Dr Wilde, its Dr Barrett, open the door."

"What on earth are you doing here? Please tell me you're not an escapee on the run?"

"I was discharged this morning, but my mother has disowned me, and I have no place else to go. Can I stay here for a while?"

"Absolutely not, my wife would strongly object to a mental patient living in our house."

"Can we not withhold that piece of information for my sake."

"It's not just my wife, what you did was unforgivable, you embarrassed me and tarnished my reputation at the university I am a laughingstock, it cannot be excused. You are going to have to arrange alternative accommodation."

"But you're my friend."

"My estimation of you has plummeted and our friendship is hanging in the balance, and quite frankly, you have to redeem yourself Dr Barrett. Until then I don't want to see you again."

"Can you spare some money?"

"You can have what's in my wallet but that's about it. Here fifty pounds it's all I have."

"Thank you, I won't bother you any longer, bye."

I moseyed along to the local convenience store bought a litre bottle of water to wash my medication down with and a pack of twelve eggs. I returned to Dr Wilde's house and pelted it with the eggs. He emerged enraged but I evaded capture, landing a direct hit on his face.

"I will get you for this Dr Barrett! Mark my word."

Due to inexperience and ignorance, I could not locate a homeless shelter opting to choose a spot of grass in Kelvingrove park to sleep on. It rained. I shivered. Some local delinquents decided to start kicking me in my sleep. I awoke and fled before they could inflict more damage. For the two weeks that followed I slept rough on the streets begging for money, instead of spending my meagre donations on food I bought pouches of rolling tobacco and smoked cigarettes – an old indulgence to appease myself, but it proved to be a costly habit that I could not sustain, so I went cold turkey to add to my destitution. Acquiring my medication was relatively simple as I was registered at my mother's address. I would visit my general practitioner who would write out a prescription which I would take to the pharmacist, due to the abolishment of charges in my country, all it took was to confirm my postcode and it would be dispensed. However, I was foolish to neglect the date I left the hospital and when it came time to visit Dr Blake, I was several days too late, but he made an exception for me.

"Dr Blake, I am living on the streets, can you help?"

"This is somewhat out of my domain. I would advise you to go to the city chambers and apply for council housing. There may be a prolonged waiting period until you're allocated a property."

"Is there no way you can assist?"

"I can but I requires a great deal of paperwork. I think this would aid your recovery if you resolved this by your own means."

"But you're my psychiatrist, I overheard nurses arranging accommodation for other patients."

"You must mean assisted living, that is a different matter altogether."

"You're not going to help me?"

"I have done all I can, I made you well didn't I? And my only obligation is to keep you that way."

"You are con, a charlatan, I renounce you, you halfwit. You can take your simpleminded methods and shove them."

I took the pills from my pocket and threw them on his desk.

"You know where these belong."

Despite warnings of the adverse effects and an increased risk of relapse at a sudden withdrawal from antipsychotics, I stopped taking the medication from that day on developing neuroleptic malignant syndrome. My fever was ferocious weakening my resolve, the tremors had me convulsing violently and my impaired consciousness ravaged my sanity. I lay in this delirious state in a doorway for a week almost succumbing to death on several occasions but no matter how I suffered I had an incessant impulse to live. When I regained my physical strength, my mental faculties didn't follow suit. I saw Dr Schultz, Click, Click, Buzz, Click, Click, Buzz, Zing, Robert, Jimmy, the stranger in the car. I saw them all, those who died by my hand, down alleyways, on street corners, they plagued me, yet I felt no remorse, it was apparent to me that this torment was a crisis of conscience originating from an inherent weakness. I ran through the streets yelling that the dead have risen there is no salvation unless we herald in a new revolution against those that oppress us, these ghastly apparitions. I spat at people's feet in contempt for they too haunted my dreams.

"What are you looking at I am the insurrection."

"Did you just spit on my husband's shoe?"

"I believe I did."

"Don't do it Arthur, I will call the police."

"We are already here, step aside, ma'am."

"Cuff him MacLerie."

"Where are you taking me?"

"A nice, secluded area where we can talk, isn't that right MacLerie?"

"I think we should take him to the mental hospital and do him no harm."

"I am going to kill you for what you have done to my partner."

"I know just the spot officer MacGill, its out by the lake. I will direct you there."

"Please do Ethan, and for your cooperation I will make this quick."

"Pull over here. Follow me on foot."

"Where are you taking us Ethan?"

"I don't rightly know."

"That's it, get on your knees."

"Did they issue you that pistol?"

"I borrowed it from our firearms unit. Any last words?"

At that moment, staring down the barrel of a gun I had an epiphany…

"That's why I brought you here…"

I hyper-physically moved MacGill's arm a fraction upwards.

"Oh my god, what have I done I've shot MacLerie."

MacLerie who was standing directly behind me fell to the ground. MacGill dropped the gun on the ground and ran over to administer his first aid training, which amounted to applying pressure on the wound.

"I'm so sorry MacLerie, I didn't mean to, it was that witch."

"I am in no way gender fluid MacGill, but that I can excuse, as for your attempt to execute me…"

157

I picked up the gun and shot MacGill twice in back. I then walked over to MacLerie who was gasping for air haven been shot in the lung.

"Your degrading assault was a cinch in comparison, do you submit MacLerie? Do you acknowledge me as your despotic superior?"

MacLerie's response was to gurgle blood, so I fired a round off into his head to put him out of his misery.

"I smell toasted bacon."

I dragged their bodies to the police car, drove for an hour, turned down a dirt track, tore off MacLerie's sleeve and fed it into the fuel tank. With the lighter I still possessed from my nicotine relapse I set the cloth on fire and watched from a suitable distance as it made its way to the filler neck, it ignited, and the car exploded in a fiery inferno, incinerating all within. I made my way through the forest as not to be apprehended for this heinous double murder. I did not ease off my pace as I walked to the lake, from there I headed to its last known location.

Chapter 7
Empiricism

"Dr Wilde, open the door, I no longer doubt my sanity and I have a method, which is quite simple really, to persuade you of what I say is true."

"How dare you show your face here again. Barbra get some eggs."

"Are you going to do what I think you are?"

"I will give you a head start Dr Barrett, out of courtesy."

"Here are the eggs darling."

"Dr Wilde won't be needing those, will you Dr Wilde?"

"Barbra put the eggs away I have an important discussion to have with Dr Barrett."

"Now I have egg on my face, darling."

"Away with you woman, do accompany me to the sitting room Dr Barrett."

"Thank you for the tea, Barbra."

"Pleasure, Dr Barrett. Your being dreadfully quiet darling and your eyes look awfully vacated."

"I've just had a great idea. Why don't we invite some of our friends from the university out to the log cabin to hear Dr Barrett's lecture again. They can bring their spouses and children as well. It will be a family retreat with an intellectual undertone. What do you say, wifey? Why are you winking at me?"

Barbara whispered into Dr Wilde's ear. I overheard the word 'joke'.

"I have since changed my mind."

"Oh, okay then that sounds delightful darling. I have been waiting for a social occasion for such a long time. Oh, I could wear my flowery frock and…"

"This is not ballroom we are going to it's the rustic outdoors."

"Sorry darling, I will wear the appropriate attire."

"That is all, away with you. I will get it organised. Dr Barrett is going to stay with us until then. No objections, I don't want to hear it."

Two weeks later, the car loaded with luggage, and I with the honour of being in the passenger seat and Barbara relegated to the back, we set off with a shifting stream of consciousness to rendezvous with the scientific scouting party at the log cabin.

"How are we all supposed to stay in this log cabin there is not enough beds?"

"Valid point Dr Thompson but all will be revealed after Dr Barrett's keynote speech."

"That's right follow me... What are you discussing amongst yourselves?"

"Well Dr Barrett, none of us know how we mysteriously ended up in the forest. The last thing we can recall was being in the log cabin waiting patiently for your opening remarks."

"Dr Thompson, my speech was so enthralling and compelling that I convinced you all to trek through the forest to show you something of great importance."

"Very well, lead on. Come on everyone were following Dr Barrett."

"Now ladies and gentlemen, gather round, what I am about to show you will amaze and astound, altering your very perception of reality and cause you to question your inflated status as a human in the universe."

"Gather round everyone Dr Barrett is going to perform a magic trick."

"It does sound like he's a magician Dr Irvine."

"That's why is said it Dr Williamson."

"Words don't do it justice, but I will give an anecdotal account to provide some context. Everyone sit down and get comfortable."

The flock did as I said, and I conditioned their minds with a verbatim recitation of my lecture for approximately thirty minutes, repetitively, inducing their receptive minds to adhere to my will.

"Now for the great reveal, prepare to be astonished."

I opened the ramp to the spacecraft, pulled the cloaking device lever and walked outside.

"Abracadabra, Dr Irvine. The look on your faces."

They stood stunned by the spacecraft momentarily. Confronted by a mechanical phenomenon of a superior race the instinct of flight took hold and they turned on their heels to flee, with the exception of Dr Irvine to my surprise.

"They outrival us, run away."

"We must retreat, the extra-terrestrials have the upper hand."

"They are going to invade earth."

"They are going to probe us."

"Quickly save the woman and children."

"Every man for himself."

"Where are you all going? We must immediately start a dialogue with these preeminent entities… We come in peace."

"That's the spirit Dr Irvine."

"I suggest you stay out of this Dr Barrett, you maladroit. I have the required sapience to mediate this encounter."

For those who recoiled in horror at their inferiority, I infiltrated their conscious once more with a hyperphysical command, to convert their cowardly mentality into a courageous state and confront the situation. They hesitantly returned compelled by some counterintuitive reasoning. Abjectly petrified, the group stood in anticipation of some sort of explanation as to why they're not fleeing.

"Remember ladies and gentlemen I reduced them to ash and bone, and this here is an alien artifact from an extinct civilisation, an extra-terrestrial spacecraft. It truly is an innovation of aerospace engineering."

"So, they are not going to attack?"

"Do recall the lecture, you fearless bunch."

"I am sorry I ever doubted you Dr Barrett."

"You have my gratitude Dr Wilde, all is forgiven."

"The Arachnids must have been very intelligent to have built that, Dr Barrett, principally that cloaking device its remarkable."

"Yes, they were bright, especially Click, Click, Buzz."

"You eradicated them because they imprisoned you? Quite frankly, I would take the exact same measure when it comes to you Dr Barrett, and thus your response was disproportionate and unethical. You are a genocidal murderer."

"Dr Irvine, clearly you have a problem with me, but I had to take pre-emptive measures, despite my intentions and my emphasis on diplomacy, they considered humanity to be an incidental epidemic, altogether expendable in relation to their enterprise – to acquire land and resources for their ever-growing population."

"How exactly did you defeat an alien race?"

"That is confidential depending on the impression you make, Dr Thompson."

"You have destroyed an ally; the synergetic knowledge surpasses any conflict; they too would have known this. You are a murderer. Come on everyone find a rope and we will lynch him."

"Dr Irvine be reasonable, he had to prioritise his own species and I think it's unbelievable that you acquired humanity a new planet, you are a hero and a saviour, in my humble opinion."

"Thank you, Dr Thompson. I am glad you see it that way."

"Why is no one listening to me, we were alone in the universe until now, we would have a better chance at survival had we cooperated with a unified objective. That is why peace would have prevailed and thus we must punish Dr Barret with death."

The congregation began to discuss it amongst themselves. I could infer opinion was divided.

"Those who think I did wrong stand to the left and if you consider me to be in the right, well stand to the right."

A third of the group stood to the left.

"I didn't account for such a divergence but easily solved."

"I have a question. None of the worlds in our galaxy are habitable, except earth, Dr Barrett, it would take approximately one hundred and ten million years to reach the edge of our galaxy."

"One word to explain this Dr Zhou, 'wormhole' near Saturn. They discovered it by monitoring orbiting stars to see if there are perturbations."

"That is a purely theoretical notion, mere speculation Dr Barrett, and if it were to exist our astronomers would have discovered it."

"I can't explain what 'exotic' matter has led to its existence and stability, and why it's gone unnoticed, but I can prove it's there."

"You can't explain very much, Dr Barrett, and yet we have unwittingly followed you into his nightmare, and I don't know why."

"Enough Dr Williamson, stop behaving like a child."

"Hey, I'm a child."

"No offence intended Hamish. Now go back and cower with the other children behind that bush."

"I'm not scared of aliens; I've seen them on the television. They're little green creatures."

"Not these aliens, they are big and terrifying. Six legs and an armour crusted body with large canines perfect for gobbling up a child."

"Stop it Dr Barrett, you're scaring the children."

"Now as I said in my speech, everyone in the spacecraft so we can depart for Planet Arachne."

"Wait one minute Dr Barrett, I have no intention of boarding that spacecraft and undertaking an intergalactic voyage."

"I on the contrary, Dr Irvine, as a scientist, cannot pass up this opportunity to survey a new planet. I will happily join you Dr Barrett."

"But you don't have a family Dr Thompson. Think of the children."

I permitted a long tedious debate to ensue which got very heated, topics of discussion were interstellar emigration, lifestyle conditions of this new environment, hostile lifeforms in an alien ecosystem, what we would survive on; the sacrifice of their hard-earned possessions, the separation from their friends and family, who would take care of their affairs back on earth, and above all else the duration of the odyssey.

"Enough chatter, I am going to take action."

Dr Irvine charged at me, but Dr Thompson and Dr Wilde restrained him.

"I will get you, Dr Barrett, mark my word."

"Terrifying…I am inclined to leave you behind Dr Irvine, but you have seen too much, so I will suppress your maniacal urges with interpolated reason."

"You'll do what now?"

"That's it I am going straight my councillor, Wilfred Ainsworth, to inform him of the discovery so he can bing it to the attention of elected members of the national party so they can instigate an emergency cabinet meeting to ascertain what to do."

"What do the first minister and her contingent of politically motivated cronies have the capacity for? Do they have the mentality and composure to do what we can?"

"The government, Dr Barrett, have the might and wealth of an entire nation compared to our measly entourage."

"I have a better solution; I know the chief executive for the Unitit Kinrick Space Agency, they will have protocols for such an improbable scenario."

"Yes, it will be to share this discovery with the international community."

"Nothing wrong with that, Dr Barrett, it should be a matter for the United Nations."

"I doubt it, they will probably contain, isolate and classify the incident preventing any hysteria caused from reaching the public domain."

"Everyone, breath and listen to your mind."

"Were trying to have a serious conversation here, Dr Barrett."

"What you are discussing is utterly meaningless, given that it is my discovery."

"You can't call shotgun on this, Dr Barrett."

"I will decide the particulars of the plan and you will blindly follow."

"Over my dead body, Dr Barrett. I must see Wilfred."

With a cunning incentive introduced to their susceptible minds, repeatedly, we all boarded the spacecraft, fired up the fuselage thruster to get airborne and ignited the full plasma propellant repertoire to blast us out of the earth's atmosphere.

"I hope there is no one from the flat Earth society on board."

"Wow."

"It's beautiful."

"Incredible."

"Nothing I haven't seen in pictures."

"You must be joking Dr Irvine; how can you be so impervious to such a spectacular view?"

"He is a bitter old fool, ignore him, Dr Thompson."

"Let's just say I am hard to impress, Dr Wilde."

Claustrophobia arrested the crew confined to the spaceship for years. Solidarity eroded and tension began to rise in the ranks until a full-scale disparity surfaced. I had to address the assembly and purge the group of any animosity.

"Dear fellow astronauts, you have displayed admirable tolerance with each other in this tight confinement on what is a long journey. The high standard of conduct is exemplary but nothing that I didn't expect from such an intelligent and distinguished group of scientists and their well nurtured families. However, I am concerned that our nerves are beginning to get frayed. I appeal to the decency you bestow and remind everyone what our true goal is. With this in mind, I ask of you to treat each other with respect and courtesy. If arguments do arise, I ask you to resolve them in a gracious manner, and I appeal to you now to maintain a certain decorum for the duration of the flight. We are a heterogeneous group of borderline arrogant professors, and that stubborn quality is no less present in your families but even a cantankerous fool can be taught tolerance or enlightened through mindfulness. I estimate that we have only a year and a half to go so do remain patient and civil. Thank you."

All of a sudden, a voice appeared from the back.

"Who put you in charge?"

"Excuse me who said that? Please come forward."

A man gradually pushed his way through the crowd.

"Please introduce yourself. I am sure everyone is eager to know who you are."

"But they know me."

I cleared my throat for affect and to indicate what I expect.

"Okay, hello, my name is Dr Irvine."

"Everyone say hello to Dr Irvine."

"Hello, Dr Irvine."

I allowed this dissension as a therapeutic exercise, catharsis if you will. A discharge of emotions is perhaps just what this group needs.

"Now what seems to be the problem?"

"I was just wondering who put you in charge?"

"Now Dr Irvine, I am not in charge. I was merely addressing the group to keep up morale. You must understand?"

"I suppose I understand but you said it with an air of authority. That's what bothered me."

"We are all equal here Dr Irvine. No one is a figure of authority. The key component of our new society is equality. We are a democracy were rights and privileges are shared equally. There is no elected body to make our decisions, so we will put everything to the vote. The majority rules."

"Are you patronizing me?"

Oh yes, the tyranny of the many opposing the individual once again, but I have already contemplated ethics and decided to at least give them some freedom, their basic rights will be sustained.

"Do you all agree with this?"

They all began to discuss what I had said.

"If there are any objections, please raise your hand?"

Not a single insubordinate raised their hand. It appears my reinforcement training was not in vain.

"You are doing it again Dr Barrett, who elected you speaker?"

"Okay, Dr Irvine please address the group."

"Okay everyone, I am not much of a public speaker, but let's form a tribunal; you all will adopt the role of the jury and I will act as judge, and we will decide the fate of Dr Barrett. If found guilty we will execute him for war crimes."

"How do you plan to operate the spacecraft without me?"

"I am sure I can learn."

"And you plan to continue the journey to Planet Arachne?"

"Absolutely not, we will return to earth and expose you."

"What do you plan to do with this new planet?"

"That is a matter for the government and for the people of our nation to form a collective democratic judgement."

The group defected once more to Dr Irvine's cause and began discussing amongst themselves. Quarrelling, in fact, about my trial and the return to earth. Finally, someone let their opinion be known.

"No one will face the guillotine under my watch. The death penalty has been outlawed for a reason. But I do concur with Dr Irvine on one point, I think we should return to earth."

"Please come forward and introduce yourself."

"Hello, my name is Dr Williamson. I am unwilling to sacrifice comfort for exploration. I recently bought a new house that my family have settled in, and we were looking to spend the rest of our lives there; in that neighbourhood and raise our children."

"Dr Williamson, we won't have the amenities or conveniences on earth, but I am sure we can adapt to the deficient in what is requisite. Plus, we will transport those skilled in crafts who can help us build houses, sewage, and irrigation systems et cetera."

"Yes, Dr Barrett but that won't be for years to come what are we supposed to do in the meantime?"

"As nature intended, Dr Williamson."

"That isn't very reassuring. I want to return to earth. Who is with me?"

"Hello, I am Dr Thompson. I quite frankly would love to go to this alien planet. It appeals to the adventurer in me and from a scientific standpoint this is a discovery that we can't overlook for comfort."

"I agree with Dr Thompson. How could we as scientists dismiss this opportunity for a lifestyle? Think of the atypical ecosystem, the numerous undocumented species. We can even verify if the laws of nature apply to this unique environment. However, the proliferation of humanity is the main objective, establishing a colony adhering to a socialist doctrine, therefrom transporting skilled labourers for the amelioration of the living conditions of our community. As our society advances and grows then we may think of altering to a manageable capitalist regime but for now everything remains in the public domain as our socioeconomic development is in its infancy. The acquisition of knowledge of Planet Arachne is secondary but no less important hence why I brought scientists."

"So that's your grand plan… communism… He's a soviet spy. Kill him."

"What's wrong with communism?"

"Ignore him, Dr Zhou."

Dr Irvine made a dash for the alien's weaponry on the gun rack, he picked one up and held it in my direction. I approached him slowly until the gun was pressed against my forehead.

"Do you have it in you to kill someone Dr Irvine? It takes a particular kind of psychopath for this undertaking."

"I am going to press the trigger, Dr Barrett."

He held the gun as he began to tremble, his finger twitched upon the trigger.

"On your knees Dr Irvine."

He did as I said to the astonishment of the group. I hyperphysically maneuvered him as to point the gun at his head.

"Dr Barrett, stop, please, stop."

Dr Thompson ran over and kicked the gun out of Dr Irvine's hands.

"I don't know what is happening here, but enough, the two of you."

The gathered crowd questioned why he had turned the gun upon himself.

"Okay, everyone, the melodrama for the time being is over. Dr Irvine is mind is clearly disordered, he doesn't know what he is doing, so everyone give him some space so he can rest."

His wife went over to console him, scowling at me all the while, as he curled upon on the hard surface of the floor that we had all been having restlessly sleeping on over the course of the journey.

"Dr Barrett, I have a concern."

"I too have a concern."

"Me too."

"One at a time, Dr Williamson you first."

"Do you expect us to live outside like animals?"

"Luckily for you Williamson, we will briefly stay in a bunker high up in the mountains with all the provisions we need, and then we will venture outside when the time is right, to the equator; to a warmer climate where we will setup camp. It will be fairly basic at first but if we all work together, we can improve it over time."

"What is in this ominous bunker?"

"A medical bay, a pantry of sorts, decontamination room, storage area for the spacecraft fuel, landing bay, observatory, sleeping chambers and a varying assortment of other rooms."

"So, there is beds? I must stipulate this condition as sleeping on a hard surface is untenable."

"That's what you derived from that... Due to the Arachnid's anatomical structure, they had no need for beds, but we can create one using their medical overalls which should suffice."

"Tell them about the nuclear weapons Dr Barrett?"

"Dr Thompson, I told you that in confidence. Fear not expedition crew the aliens were neutralised, and the weapons are secure."

"What else haven't you told us?"

"In the context of nuclear energy... they have reactors stationed throughout the land. It is their exclusive source of energy. Although humanity has developed this technology, the Arachnid's were quite ingenious in how they harnessed thermal energy to generate electricity. My intention is to redirect the current from their substation along the high-voltage transmission lines, so we have functioning electric power grid to power our encampment. I have extensive knowledge of nuclear reactors and can easily facilitate this."

"Is that why Dr Scholtz jovially referred to you as the Atomic Savant?"

"He should have known better than to mention that to a friend, however trusted, but he did always court controversy, Dr Wilde."

"You never shy from controversy Dr Barrett... I on the other hand want to decommission the nuclear power plants and implement an organic source; in particular, renewable energy. I also want to nominate myself as president of this syndicate."

"Is that so, Dr Irvine."

"Have you considered what to do with the spent fuel; the waste materials, Dr Barrett?"

"Dispose of it on an uninhabitable planet within the galaxy, that's what the Arachnids did."

"You consider this to be morally correct?"

"I consider it to be pragmatic."

"This is a rather divisive topic, perhaps we should put it to the vote? Raise your hand if you subscribe to Dr Barrett's unique brand of insanity?"

Three quarters of the crew concurred with Dr Irvine's proposal.

"I should expect no less from the whims of the mob."

"You should be gracious in defeat, Dr Barrett."

"You underestimate me, Dr Irvine, this is only the beginning of the feud."

"I have a question for you Dr Irvine, where are the engineers to construct wind turbines, solar panels and what have you?"

"We will immediately return to earth to recruit those skilled in engineering, Dr Zhou."

"You do not wish to adhere to a democratic vote or Dr Thompson's plan to inform the space agency? Or perhaps Dr Huxley's councillor?"

"I have since changed my mind, I wish for this to remain a secret, I will establish a transport network to this planet for vast sums of money, all very covert, only available to the truly rich. I will be a billionaire in no time. Then my wife and I will move to Monaco where I will reside with tax exemptions all the while overseeing the development of society on this new planet. When the living conditions are finally worthy of my presence I will move to a mansion and retire. Of course, everyone here is welcome to a share in my enterprise. It will be known as 'Irvine the Divine Club and Resort Ltd'."

"You vulgarian, you are looking to monetise and profit off this discovery, to diminish it to a tourist attraction."

"Yes, Dr Barrett, I will elevate this place to a desirable upper-class destination otherwise it will remain derelict and abandoned."

"So that will be your immigration policy, super rich?"

"Yes, Dr Thompson."

"Irrespective of how developed our living conditions are people will want to come and I certainly will not discriminate based on wealth, anyone is welcome who has a required skill that they can contribute to our society."

"Okay, syndicate how should we proceed? Non-profit or profit-making business?"

The expedition crew could not decide on which approach to take.

"You are corrupting my crew Dr Irvine, and I will not stand for this."

Dr Irvine dashed for the alien weaponry, but Dr Wilde and Dr Thompson were a step ahead restraining him from inflicting damage upon me, not that I needed their intervention, but it restored peace momentarily.

"I have a pertinent question."

"Go ahead Dr Zhou."

"Dr Irvine seems intent on killing you what if he succeeds or if there is another violation of common law?"

"We will adopt a self-regulated civilian law enforcement to regulate behaviour, whereby any transgressions and the offender will be locked up in solitary confinement and then banished back to planet earth."

"Their punishment is to return to earth? I think we are all willing to commit a crime for that."

"Let's be reasonable, you are upstanding citizens who will always choose the right course of action based upon your intellect and moral capacity. You are scientists not criminals."

By the time the planet Arachne had come into the horizon I had subjugated my fellow travellers beyond reproach. But I rationalised that this would benefit the greater number of people.

"That expedition crew, as you may have realised, is planet Arachne."

"Finally, I couldn't take any more years in tedium."

"Let's hope it's as hospitable as you say for therein lies your redemption, Dr Barrett."

A palpable buzz of excitement filled the interior of the spacecraft.

Chapter 8
The Colony

A commotion came from the expedition crew as I approached atmospheric re-entry.

"Dr Barrett, please reassure us that you have the capability of entry without incinerating us all?"

"Were you not paying attention to the exothermic display when we left the earth's atmosphere?"

"I have no recollection, Dr Barrett. It's the damndest thing, I seem to go from one event to the next without being conscious of it happening."

"Fine, Dr Thompson, it occurred to me that the Arachnids were aware of a simple engineering principle that the aerodynamic heating experienced by the spacecraft is inversely proportional to the drag coefficient. The atmospheric drag created by a larger blunt surface area traps the air creating a cushion which deflects the heated shock layer away from the spacecraft greatly reducing the mechanical stresses. Hence why the mid-fuselage is taking the brunt."

"We are protected by drag force?"

"Not entirely, Dr Zhou, I could image the spacecraft has been reinforced."

"Nothing will sufficiently comfort me with you at the helm, Dr Barrett."

"The feeling is mutual, Dr Irvine."

We hurtled through what I have designated as Planet Arachne's mesosphere given the build-up of flames.

"Is that normal Dr Barrett?"

Without the displacement of the crew and safe in the knowledge that most of the kinetic energy had dissipated into heat, I initiated the thrusters until the spacecraft was suspended securely above the ground. To illicit a further understanding of my combative approach I set off to my strategic stronghold, taking the opportunity to demonstrate my piloting skills. I flew into a deep ravine much to the consternation of the crew.

"Is it really necessary to show off, Dr Barrett? Especially when you are risking our lives."

I pressed forward and ascended. I came to a valley with a massive crater and the surrounding area decimated.

"What happened here?"

"The aliens dropped nuclear bombs on the compound I was in, Dr Thompson."

"Ah I see, but I presume you too had a nuclear arsenal at their disposal from inside that bunker. That's how you were victorious?"

"No, I didn't have nuclear weapons. I utilised something far more effective."

"What can be more effective in war than an atomic bomb?"

"That shall remain a secret for the time being."

I pressed on to the bunker in the mountainous region.

"I don't believe it…"

"What's wrong Dr Barrett?"

"I left the landing bay door open."

"Someone or something closed it? Oh, my goodness, we should retreat, Dr Barrett."

"It seems illogical, but I must have closed it from the inside, the idiot that I am."

I landed the spacecraft precariously on the edge of the mountain.

"How did you fly out if its sealed shut?"

"I don't know."

"How are we supposed to get in? This looks like steel doors – they could be a metre thick or more. We don't have any dynamite to blow them open, depending on the thickness of course."

"Just wait."

With the absence of a host an aspect of my hyperphysical proved useless so I resorted to my telekinesis. I imagined myself passing through the door, and surprisingly it was if I could see through a pair of eyes at the other end. From what I saw there was a key card deliberately placed right at the entrance. Several hours passed as I toiled with the key card, the others took it upon themselves to throw rocks at the steel door, they tired of this and started discussing other matters. It became obvious that I couldn't do it. I became disillusioned. I wandered over to the edge of the cliff and stared down at the precipice below me.

"Steel door dumbfounded you Dr Barrett?"

They all started laughing. I went into a furious rage.

"This is merely a setback, but it won't impede me for much longer."

"Here Dr Barrett have a rock."

They all started laughing again. By this time, I was embodied with anger. I passed through the steel door, approached the key card, plucked it off the ground and scanned it on the locking mechanism which opened the door.

"That is incredible Dr Barrett, how did you do that?"

"I think he willed it open."

Again, they were laughing. I wasn't amused.

"You really were between a rock and a hard place their Dr Barrett."

"Shut up and follow me."

We walked into the compound and started to look around.

"In all seriousness Dr Barrett, how did you open the door?"

They all gathered round eagerly awaiting my response.

"Let me guess you had a remote control this whole time and you were just messing with us?"

"I will tell you when I think you're ready Dr Thompson."

"He's a trickster and a charlatan, he had a remote control."

"This place is amazing though."

"Don't touch anything."

"What's through that door, Dr Barrett?"

"It takes you to the launching area for the nuclear warheads. We will be avoiding that indefinitely."

"I noticed medical equipment and what seems like various medicines; however, there is no descriptive label, not that I could translate their symbolic language. What I am trying to say is I have no idea what they are."

"What are we going to do if someone falls ill?"

"We will alleviate their symptoms the best we can."

"What are you a witch doctor now, Dr Barrett?"

"Not to worry no one will get ill."

I emerged from my disturbed sleep, hip aching from the hard floor, barely enough motivation to lift my corpse into an upright position, suspended in a half-conscious state waiting for my acute faculties to return to working order. Luckily, I had saved a cigarette precisely for the purpose of elevating the unpleasantries of life on this new world. With this luxury playing on my mind, I got to my feet, excused myself and swiftly found an empty room. I pressed my thumb against the flint but there was no movement. It had jammed. With this I went into a furious rage, held the lighter high in the sky and with a swift motion I brought my arm down intending on smashing it against the ground, but no, I must persist. I sparked the lighter, and miraculously, ignited the butane, brought the lighter to my cigarette, inhaled with all my might and drew the smoke into my lungs, a slight stimulation caused my head to feel light and my vision to blur. This wasn't a disagreeable effect, in fact this was exactly what I had in mind, and I was instantly relaxed. The day in front of me came into focus and I assimilated a plan from fragments of memory.

I burst into the room with renewed vigour,

"Good morning, ladies and gentlemen. How are we all today?"

Silence.

"Not all at once, save that energy for more productive exploits."

"Why are you so happy? Have you got used to sleeping on the ground?"

"On the contrary, my hip is killing me. If only I keep sleep on my back instead of my side. Today we will make for the equator. Gather supplies."

The sleep deprived crew followed me into the spacecraft expressing their distaste for the bunker. I told them to submit their complaints with our chief administrative officer Dr Thompson, much to his dismay. We crammed the spacecraft with provisions and made haste.

"Okay this is the spot."

I set down the spacecraft and we disembarked.

"Look at the bones."

"That would be the Arachnids."

"This heat is stifling."

"I find this to be an optimal temperature plus its better than the cold."

"Your preferences are prejudiced by your motives, Dr Barrett."

The first evening was a mixture of fear and irritation.

"These bugs are eating me alive."

"Some of them are alarmingly big."

"Just swat them away."

"How? That one is as big as a cat."

"Ouch, something stung me… and now my leg is throbbing with pain."

"Let me have a look. Oh dear, that leg is going to have to be amputated."

"Are you serious?"

"What did I tell you about being so gullible Barbra? You are despicable, Dr Barrett."

"I guess my humour is not appreciated, Dr Wilde."

"What's that noise…? It is coming from the bushes over there."

"It's not even in close proximity to us."

"How can you be sure, Dr Barrett?"

"Look a flock of, erm, alien birds…"

"Why are they flocking this way…? Ahh take cover."

"They are only inquisitive."

"Nothing will comfort in this appalling place. I may as well be in purgatory."

This continued into the darkness of night and by the time it was dawn we had been mauled by insects.

"We have no insect repellent nor ointment. What are we going to do?"

"We should return to the bunker tonight."

"We must adapt and survive outside so bear with it."

"I am developing bruxism because of you, Dr Barrett."

The next day I organised along with Dr Zhou an exploration party to survey the area for cultivated land to pilfer the Arachnid's crops. The ones that remained sunbathed, eating our unappetising rehydratable food, and sipping from the containers of water. Our supplies at the camp were sparse but I could return to the bunker's stocked pantry if need be.

"We should consider hunting some of the animals for sustenance?"

"What if we get food poisoning? We have no idea if our digestive system will tolerate the meat. Furthermore, it could be toxic, like a defence mechanism."

"Okay, we will kill one and assess if it is flavoursome, and more importantly if it is safe. Let's arm ourselves."

Brandishing the laser guns relinquished from the grip of the Arachnid's lifeless remains, we set off in a set formation covering all angles. We came to the edge of what appeared to be a tropical jungle.

"Should we venture in there?"

"I don't see why not we are equipped with weaponry, Dr Thompson."

Struggling our way through the undergrowth, I heard a very loud rustling sound from through the thicket and a snarl accompanied by the panicked chatter of the other members of our scouting party. I shouted to regroup.

"What was that Dr Barrett?"

"I don't know, who's missing?"

"Dr Irvine."

"Let's search for him."

We found Dr Irvine on the ground with clawing marks on his stomach and his throat torn out.

"Some sort of creature has killed Dr Irvine."

"Stop shouting Dr Williamson, you will encourage it to come back. Dr Barrett, take off your jumper and help me stop the haemorrhaging."

"This jumper has sentimental value. He is dead anyway there is nothing we can do for him."

"A little compassion, Dr Barrett."

"Our hope died with that man."

"Don't be so melodramatic, Dr Williamson."

"Dr Irvine had vision… How do you propose to get us out of this situation, Dr Barrett?"

"If the beast shall return, we will kill it with our laser guns."

"We're doomed."

"Someone help me carry his body."

"No, Dr Thompson, he will slow us down, we will be an easier target carrying him."

"A little respect for the dead, Dr Barrett."

"I agree, Dr Thompson, we can't leave his corpse to rot."

"Put him down we can always come back for his body and give him a proper burial."

"I have to agree with you Dr Barrett, he is rather heavy."

"What are we going to tell his wife?"

"We are going to have to tell her the truth."

"She will be distraught; her husband has just been killed, and you Dr Barrett, are culpable for his death, irresponsibly leading us into mortal danger, you egotistical fascist."

"There is no need to insult me, Dr Williamson, he was well aware of the danger involved, although, I didn't except any fatalities, but now that it has happened, we can only honour his death for the sacrifice he has made. He gave his life for the cause to bring humanity one step closer…"

"Let's go back to the camp to discuss this further before anyone else is killed."

Everyone was in complete agreement with Dr Thompson including myself, given how cunning these animals were even I was in danger. I had my doubts I could possess them before they struck killer blow. Gingerly walking through the forest we saw something flash by us, we all instinctively shot at it.

"Okay, okay, cease fire."

"What the hell was that?"

"I'm terrified."

"Come on gain composure, Dr Williamson. We have this under control."

"What are you talking about, Dr Barrett? That thing is too fast to even aim at. Were screwed."

"We need to get it out into the open. We are too vulnerable in this bloody jungle. Let's just make a run for it. Okay, on the count of three. One, two, three… run, run, run."

We fled with such conviction and speed that we almost lost each other. Despite our best effort we were still in the jungle, exhausted from our exertion.

"Well, that didn't work."

All of a sudden, we heard a rustling in the bushes.

"Oh damn, that thing has followed us."

"I think we should try and flush it out."

"How do you propose to do that Dr Barrett?"

"We will climb up a tree and have Dr Williamson scream at the top of his lungs. When it appears, we will shoot it."

"Eh, what? I'm not doing that."

"That won't work Dr Barrett."

"Let's give it a try."

We eventually convinced Dr Williamson to scream at the top of his lungs. We climbed into the trees and waited. By some unknown intervention, the bloody beast went for him, and I caught it's just in time with my hyperphysical ability and had it stand in one spot.

"Shoot, shoot."

At that we fired countless lasers into the beast. We climbed out the tress and examined it.

"It looks like a cat."

"They are cunning and lethal felines. But clearly not all that clever."

"Why did it just stand there?"

"I forgo recognition… maybe it was sizing him up."

"Check its pulse to make sure it's dead."

"It's dead, Dr Zhou."

We kept searching for a way out of the jungle; we climbed trees to trying to get a better view, we climbed up the side of a cliff but to no avail. We heard all sorts of noises emanating from the local wildlife. By this time, we were all getting worried as it was beginning to get dark. None of us had torches so we invested time in making a fire rather than trying to escape from this labyrinth. My lighter was ineffective, seems I exhausted it earlier in the day. We laboured with the fire by hitting two rocks together to make a spark but nothing materialised. Having given up on this we continued to force our way through the jungle. Darkness set in and we couldn't see a bloody thing. The group came to the decision, to climb up a tree and take refuge, there we would be safe. The noises continued, suddenly we heard rustling of the undergrowth.

"Oh no, what is that?"

"I hope it can't climb."

We saw a large creature pass below us, it was indiscernible from our vantage point amongst the branches, but from the sound erupting from its foul constitution I knew it was big and menacing. The scouting party were all terrified. I on the other hand, venerated the nature of the cantankerous beast safe in the knowledge that I could appropriate its feeble brain.

"Did anyone sleep?"

"No, I am near demented with insomnia."

Having all climbed down from the tree, a large group of animals began swinging form tree to tree above us. Calling to each other in a high-pitched tone.

"I think we just escaped certain death."

After scanning the trees to get a better look at these beasts, we decided to vacate the area. Before we knew it, it was dark again and we were clambering into the trees. This pattern continued from some days.

"Look it's an opening."

"What a relief."

"This looks familiar."

"At long last… finally got your bearings Dr Barrett."

"I have an inclination, Dr Zhou."

"Look at those animals there enormous."

"Yes, I have seen these before they are harmless herbivores, they roam in herds."

"Don't spook them though or you may cause a stampede."

"Let's walk around them."

"Good idea."

"Dr Thompson, what are you doing?"

"I want to get a closer look. They remind me of a long-legged rhino, but with four tusks."

"Not too close, they might trample you."

"I'll be fine."

Dr Thompson approached them with caution…

"On no, look they are chasing him."

"We are going to have to shoot them."

"No, he will evade them."

"They could kill him, Dr Barrett. We must help."

"Run Dr Thompson, run to the trees."

"That's your idea of helping, Dr Barrett."

Dr Thompson was at breakneck speed – he was practically hurdling his way to safety.

"Not that way Dr Thompson, there's more over there."

The herbivores flanked Dr Thompson and he was soon surrounded.

"What are they going to do to him?"

"Don't be so prosaic, Dr Williamson."

One of the alien rhinoceros rose up on its hind legs and was about to bring its front feet down on Dr Thompson's head.

"He's done for."

Suddenly, Dr Thompson leaped into action and ran through the beast's hind legs.

"Oh, thank god, he dodged it."

"Wait a minute, he is bringing them our way."

"Help me, help me."

I looked round and noticed that Dr Williamson and Dr Zhou were hightailing it away.

"Cowards."

"Run Dr Barrett, run you fool."

With that I turned on my heels raced after the others. After several yards we were all exhausted, but the beasts had given up chase.

"What were you thinking Dr Thompson?"

"Now that is what I call an immersive safari."

"Curiosity got the better of you, Dr Thompson."

"It nearly cost me my life."

We walked for days coming across other fascinating creatures, most of which I had seen during the great war.

"I have had it up to here, Dr Barrett. Do you even know if we are going in the right direction?"

"Just a couple more days."

"I should never have trusted you. I won't see my wife again; Dr Irvine has been killed and I am going to die in this godforsaken place. And who is the sole cause of this?"

Dr Williamson raised his laser gun and aimed it at me.

"I am going to kill you for this."

"Easy there fella, remember what you said about capital punishment, and put down the gun."

"No more words I must take action."

I hyperphysically coerced Dr Williamson drop his gun.

"Why did I drop the gun?"

"That's it. Dr Williamson no longer gets a gun. Someone take it, and quickly."

Dr Thompson picked up his gun.

"Listen Dr Williamson… It was Dr Barrett who led us here, but we all agreed to go. Yes, we were naïve and didn't fully comprehend that our lives would be at stake, but we knew that there would be some element of risk."

"I don't know why I agreed to come to this planet, Dr Thompson."

"Gentleman, I wish to have a moment alone with Dr Williamson to settle this affair."

The rest of the scouting party turned away and distracted themselves with the recollection of our encounters. Having satisfied myself that they won't notice, I rote brainwashed Dr Williamson for five minutes. I methodically focused on Dr Irvine's death to repress his compulsion to murder me. I manipulated his perception of who is responsible, by fabricating a story whereby Dr Irvine's influence on the endeavour was grossly exaggerated.

"Dr Irvine deserved to die for leading us here."

"Good man, Dr Williamson."

We journeyed for days until I found my bearings and made haste to the camp.

"Where is my husband?"

"I'm sorry to tell you, Mrs Irvine, but he has been killed. An animal attacked him when we were exploring. There was nothing we could do."

Mrs Irvine broke down and they tried to console her the best they could. She did not blame me for his death as I expected her to do; but rather, she sat silently crying to herself. I felt no remorse for that insubordinate ignoramus, nor for Mrs Irvine's bereavement, but failure did impress upon me for not safeguarding the expedition crew against inimical threats. I brought them unwittingly to a paradoxical paradise where death preys upon their every step, and I, their only means of salvation, was careless all those years ago in my own self-admiration. Ultimately, I overestimated the culling of these creatures, and the logic behind it now obscured by guilt, for I have admiration of how impeccable these predators are and the respect they deserve. In hindsight, I would have created a conservation reserve under prudent management to propagate their species; but without the proper infrastructure, my colony takes priority compelling me to maliciously destroy what I revere.

"Expedition crew gather round; I need volunteers for an important mission."

"I am not going back into that jungle, Dr Barrett."

"It involves piloting a spacecraft back to earth."

"Oh me, pick me."

"Okay, Dr Fleming."

"Why don't you teach all of us so we can leave this wretched place."

"Some will have to remain. I need to utilise space in the spacecrafts for the proletariat that will accompany us on the return journey."

"You expect us to fly back to this alien world?"

"Hence why I ask as you will have to sacrifice a considerable amount of time confined to the spacecraft."

"Relative to that spacecraft this is utopia. I am staying."

Eight members of the crew courageously nominated themselves.

"None of the woman? I don't want to be misconstrued as a misogynist."

"I have to stay with my children."

"I couldn't bear the claustrophobia again."

"Very well follow me pilots so I can debrief you."

"Good morning gentleman. It's a pleasure to chair this meeting of eager astronauts about to undertake the journey back to earth. I must emphasize the importance of two objectives we will attend to. First of all, I will teach you how to fly a spacecraft. I propose a few supervised practise runs, taking off from the bunker and landing before you attempt it unassisted. Once we arrive the real work will begin, which is the identification and procurement of suitable candidates for the purpose of building us a village. The primary duty is to liaise and collaborate on a design of our village with a civil engineer, I want to be involved in this process. Secondary you will assume the role of a general contractor to assemble a workforce, exempli gratia, electricians, plumbers et cetera. It is crucial that you asses not only their expertise in their field but also if they will fit seamlessly into our community. I must make it very clear before we depart that you only share the existence of Planet Arachne with those deemed essential to our enterprise. That means you repress the urge to dial nine, nine, nine and claim to have been abducted. Also, any elected official or government body must be avoided. This is crucial.

Each day for the next week we will spend two hours going over the finer details of the plan, the rest of the time is for recreation."

Throughout the week for fourteen hours at a set interval, the purpose of these debriefings is to hyperphysically inculcate secrecy in the crew with the exception to those deemed essential. I instilled a strict discipline to the cause and prohibited disclosure through fear of retribution should they violate the paradigm by which we will operate. One week later I announced to my landing party that it was now time to put into effect the second stage of the grand plan, the pilots knew the fate I had in store for them, so they were slightly more composed, but the wives and children were distraught, especially when I estimated the number of years they would be apart. I on the other hand had no emotional ties so I was quite unperturbed. The great plan took precedent over anything else in my life and I can't afford to get distracted with relationships. I did allow the pilots an extra day to spend with their families but when it was time to say goodbye, I put an end to the sentiments and coerced them into setting off for the spacecrafts with the exception of one, who was fast becoming the vain of my existence.

"Goodbye my love."

"Please don't leave me, I can't make it without you."

"Sorry men, but I can't go I must stay with my wife."

"I can't say that I am not disappointed but your involvement is not of great importance so we can afford to leave you with your darling wife."

"Not of great importance? How dare you! Sorry dear, but duty calls."

"George, listen to Dr Barrett, you're not needed, would you not rather stay with me?"

"Of course, dear, but I have to go with the men."

"But why George?"

"Because… duty calls. Your making me look bad dear."

"Please George."

"Okay."

"Good riddance Dr Williamson. Snivelling fool. Follow me fellow astronauts into the breach."

They started to discuss amongst themselves about how much they are going to miss their families, this I had to curtail.

"Gentlemen, enough. We have a far greater purpose than nurturing our offspring into adulthood or indulging in monogamy. I have already averted an unthinkable non-anthropogenic existential risk to humanity, but we are still confronted by a climate apocalypse, and how better to forestall a catastrophe than to have an antidote – Planet Arachne. Allowing earth to regenerate and potentially revert back to climate stability. In order to extricate humanity, I need your full cooperation. I can't do this on my own."

"I admire your ambition Dr Barrett, and of course, share your desire to follow through with this solution to prevent the extinction of humanity. I am fully committed to your plan."

"Me too, I'm not backing out now, I know the importance of this assignment."

"To the stars."

"Who said that?"

"Oh, that was me, Dr Barrett."

"Very good, Dr Fleming. Very good."

Prior to our departure I informed the colony that they should search for underground bunkers to find more provisions as the Arachnid crop had turned feral, and as a last resort hunt the wildlife. We boarded the spacecraft whilst waving farewell to the remaining expedition crew.

"Be resourceful my pioneers, remember you are the custodians of this world."

We set off for Click, Click, Buzz's bunker in the side of the mountain. Despite the separation anxiety the recurrence crew were relieved and excited about returning to earth particularly with the purpose I had in store for them.

"Okay everyone must assist me in loading the spacecraft with the high-pressure tanks of hydrogen and the cannisters of nuclear fuel. Please err on the side of caution this is radioactive material we are dealing with, and I can't afford any more casualties. They have hoist mechanisms so if we work as a team, we can have everything loaded by the end of the day."

That night we gorged on food supplies, with full stomachs, we retired to our makeshift beds on the hard floor. The sleep was less than desirable, but I felt refreshed the following morning.

"It is time for your lesson in aviation."

"I am apprehensive about this, Dr Barrett."

"Don't be concerned, Dr Zhou, I will be in the cockpit with you to intervene if necessary."

"I can't wait to take off."

"Easy there Dr Fleming, if you get to excited you are more prone to making a mistake."

We sauntered up to the landing bay and boarded one of the spacecrafts.

"Do you know what all these buttons do?"

"I was thoroughly and meticulously taught."

"What does this one do?"

"Haven't the faintest idea. Gather round everyone, there is no joystick as with our conventional aircraft but a thruster interface. I think the easiest way to learn is if I give you a quick demonstration. Okay now that you have observed how to fly who would like to go first?"

"Me, I will go first."

"Okay, Dr Fleming. Everyone out the spacecraft and clear the launching platform."

"Do you mind if I do this on my own? Your presence is putting a lot of pressure on me."

"Okay, I will disembark. Are you sure you have this? At least if I'm there I can correct your mistake if you make one."

"I'll be fine."

"Famous last words"

"You're not going to allow him to fly that thing by himself?"

"Yes, he insisted, Dr Thompson. I am not going to argue with him."

The spacecraft took off at some speed vertically and banged into the roof. The damage wasn't severe, but the noise was loud. Suddenly it took off and out of the compound, we saw it go higher and higher, then it changed course dramatically, swung from side to side and then plummeted.

"He is not going to be able to pull up."

We all watched as the spacecraft exploded on impact with the ground.

"Holy crap. There is no way he could have survived that."

"I think it pretty conclusive he's dead."

They all turned and looked at me.

"Who's next?"

"I will go next, but I am taking you down with me, Dr Barrett."

"Very prudent, Dr Huxley."

I anticipated a full day of instruction would suffice but it took two weeks before the recurrence crew were adept enough at flying the spacecraft, of course they are yet to experience flight control in a vacuum.

"Nine members of the earth recurrence crew we are ready to depart. The ingenious Dr Zhou has hardwired the communications system so we should be able to correspond during spaceflight, all through the magic of radio waves, but that's not all, he reprogrammed the command module tuning all spacecraft to the beacon signal frequency, it shall guide you to the location on earth from which we originated from. The seclusion of this area is ideal, but most importantly across the lake, beyond the forest, a farm is most likely still situated, with a vast expanse of agricultural land which will be perfect for landing our spacecraft without being detected. Round of applause for Dr Zhou."

With every journey I make back to earth I will be fast approaching the succumbing to cessation; the permeance of the unconscious abyss. I would have spent the last precious years of my life in a spacecraft, but my legacy will persevere through an inoculation of Progenicepathy in suitable candidates based on their virtue and wisdom; they will be a transmissible predictive nucleus; a function of the future, with an infinite value, prevailing the predetermining nature of the past, facilitating a new dawn of time of irrelative and unprecedented mutations and chemical processes; whilst, transcending the limitations of the host spawning an alternate phenomenon - truly omnipotent, and we will guide humanities evolution to its primary purpose, to attain immortality.